The Muddy Course
A Sugarbury Falls Mystery

by

Diane Weiner

For information, email Cozy Cat Press, cozycatpress@aol.com or visit our website at: www.cozycatpress.com

COZY CAT
P R E S S

ISBN: 978-1-946063-92-2
Printed in the United States of America

10 9 8 7 6 5 4 3 2 1

This book is dedicated to my loyal readers who inspire
me to keep churning out books!

Chapter 1

Emily tucked the cushions into the sofa, fluffed the throw pillows, and shooed Chester off the back. Then she noticed the Oreo crumbs and brushed them onto the floor. She'd been doing far too much stress eating since hearing from her mother. Henry folded the afghan and placed it neatly on the hearth.

"What can she possibly have to tell me now? It's about my sister? What's that supposed to mean?" The bright sun streaming through the window irritated her. She snapped the blinds shut. "Have you seen the lint roller?" Chester's black cat hair clung to the sofa. She tried picking it off with her fingers but her hands were anything but steady.

"It could mean anything. She's selling the house, right?"

"Yeah, now that she's on husband number three. My dad's been after her to sell for decades."

"I'll bet she was packing and found something she thinks your sister would have wanted you to have—like a diary or a piece of jewelry."

"It sounded too...I don't know, too urgent to be that. Every time I think of my sister..."

"We've been through this a million times. She wasn't a baby, and she knew how to swim."

"I was supposed to be looking out for her."

"Stop. It's been what, thirty years? Maybe she wants to redo the headstone or maybe she needs to tell you she wants to be buried beside her."

"She could have said that on the phone."

Teenager Maddy, in distressed jeans, a crop top which Emily thought showed too much tummy, and dirty blond hair pulled into a loose ponytail, sauntered into the living room. She plopped down on the sofa, and said, "Who's being buried?"

Emily swallowed, feeling as if sandpaper scraped her esophagus. "My, um..."

"Emily's sister died when she was about your age. Her mother wants to tell her something."

"I know, Dad. I was there when she got the phone call. Duh." She rolled her eyes at Henry. "Why are you scared of your mother, Emily? You never talk about her. By the way, I'm not calling her Grandma."

Emily slumped onto the sofa. "You'll see for yourself." She stood up, smoothed out her sweater, and ran her hand over her stomach. "Do I look fat in this?" The waistband of her jeans felt a bit tighter.

Henry said, "You look beautiful, like always."

"Emily, why are you so nervous? It's your own mother," said Maddy.

Emily didn't want to get into it. Her relationship with her mother had always been complicated but her sister's death virtually destroyed it. No wonder. If she'd been in her mother's shoes... She jumped. "What's that? Is it a car?" She peeked out the window, rattling the blinds. "They're here."

Emily cringed at her reflection in the entranceway mirror, sucked in her stomach, and opened the door. "Mom. How was your trip?"

She gave Emily an air kiss on each cheek. Emily recognized the familiar scent of Shalimar, still overpowering.

"Tiring, but we're here now." Frances wrapped her hands around the forearm of the stately gentleman beside her. "This is Drew, short for Andrew. Drew Robinson."

The irony of her mother now being Mrs. Robinson didn't escape her. Drew, clean-shaven and wearing a leather jacket with a plaid scarf, looked closer to her own age than to her mother's.

Henry stepped forward. "Nice to meet you, Drew. Good to see you again, Frances. Welcome to Vermont and congratulations on your marriage."

"Mom, Drew, this is our daughter, Maddy." She still felt her skin tingle whenever she said the word *daughter*.

"Maddy. Fiona's daughter." Her eyes scanned from the top of Maddy's blond head to the neon blue toenails that peeked through her sandals. "Is it short for Madelyn or is it just Maddy? People do that nowadays—put a nickname right on the birth certificate."

"It's Madelyn, but everyone calls me Maddy."

"I never thought I'd see the day I'd be a grandmother. Frankly, it's hard to imagine Fiona having a child, may she rest in peace." She turned to Maddy. "Your mother was what we used to call a free spirit." She seemed to react to Maddy's expression. "Lovely, though. Always a warm smile on her face. She made a wise decision naming Emily as guardian."

Emily's stomach knotted. Yes, thanks to losing her sister, she had been adamant about remaining childless when she first met Henry. She never told anyone that years later, when in retrospect it was too late, she and Henry had embraced the idea of parenthood and tried unsuccessfully to have a baby of their own.

Henry said, "Technically, you're more of a step grandmother or a surrogate…adoptive…"

"It doesn't matter what you call it," said Maddy. "I'm Fiona's daughter. And I'm your daughter's daughter. Period."

That's my girl. "I made iced tea," said Emily. Maddy referring to her as her mother warmed her skin like sunshine. Henry became *Dad* pretty quickly, while she was still, understandably, Emily. "And Maddy and I baked a banana bread. Sit down."

"I'll get it," said Maddy.

"Thanks, honey. Mom, what do you have to tell me about Amy? I've been trying to guess since that phone call."

"I...I can't quite believe it. It's a miracle. I never imagined, well, hoped, but never thought..."

"Please, spit it out." She imagined her arm reaching in and ripping the words out of her mother's mouth.

"I'm trying not to overreact. You know we never found Amy's body in that current. And then the hurricane..."

"Hurricane?" said Maddy. She set the pitcher and banana bread on the coffee table.

"Yes, just two days after Amy drowned. Emily was supposed to be watching her."

"She was my age, right?" said Maddy.

"What are you, fourteen?"

"Almost fifteen."

"Yes, fourteen. She had Down's syndrome. Her judgement, well...She had an attraction to water, yet she couldn't swim."

Emily felt her face burning from the inside. Years of therapy hadn't brought her to the point where she could forgive herself. "She wandered off. It only takes a second." Henry scooted closer and squeezed his wife's hand.

Frances said, "Emily's friends showed up. She was distracted."

"Do we have to rehash this yet again?" said Emily. "Did they find a body? I suppose by now it'd be bones. Did they find her bones? Is that why you're here?"

"No, honey, but there's been, let's call it a development."

"What are you talking about?"

"Good thing you're sitting. I nearly fainted when I heard the news. There's a possibility Amy didn't drown that day."

"Didn't drown? I saw her cap floating in the water. The current was fierce. What are you saying?"

"I saw a news article in the local paper. A young woman was kidnapped in New York, only 30 miles from where we lived in Westbrook."

"What's this have to do with Amy?"

"This woman escaped after a few days and... you won't believe this."

"What, Mom?"

"She told the police there was a woman living at the house where she was being held. A woman with 'some kind of mental condition' is how she put it."

"And you think it was Amy? It was thirty years ago and this woman was kidnapped a few days ago?"

"More than a few days, but that's beside the point. The victim said the woman living in the house was in her forties with blond hair and a scar on her left hand."

"Lots of people have blond hair, and scars for that matter. There was no one else in the woods that day— only my two friends."

"The scar was in the shape of a boxing glove. Remember when Amy burned her hand on the stove? The scar looked like a boxing glove. It has to be her."

Henry said, "Maybe they can do a DNA test."

"They haven't been able to find them yet. The victim was disoriented and the police haven't found the cabin."

"I don't see how Amy could have been abducted without me noticing. She would have screamed or something. I would have noticed."

"Emily, I'm convinced it's her." She grabbed Emily's hands. "Can you imagine? What if our prayers have been answered? What if Amy's still alive." She sobbed dramatically into Emily's shoulder.

Drew said, "We hope the police find her alive. If he had to flee, the man may have dumped her or worse."

Frances looked up from Emily's shoulder. "How dare you say that? My daughter's alive. I feel it."

Henry said, "What do the police say? Is the victim credible?"

"Why would she not be credible? Makes me so angry. The police aren't taking me seriously. They're after the kidnapper but they don't seem to care if he has Amy with him."

Henry said, "Did you get to talk to the victim?"

"The police are keeping her identity a secret. They say she may still be in danger, you know, if the kidnapper decides to come after her."

Henry said, "Our friends Susan and Mike have a daughter who's a detective in Westbrook. Maybe we can talk to her."

"That would be great. I went to the Westbrook police but they said it wasn't in their jurisdiction."

Henry said, "At this point, it may have been handed over to the FBI, especially if they think he crossed state lines."

"She's alive, I know it."

"Mom, you can't get your hopes up like that." Emily's heart pounded against her chest. What if her mother was right? What if Amy really was alive? What she'd give to hear Amy's voicing calling her Em&Em. She didn't dare hope.

Frances said, "I'm really beat from the trip." She stood up and held onto the back of the couch, then pinched a few strands of black fur between her fingers. "Do you have a cat?"

"We have a cat. His name is Chester." Maddy called Chester but he stayed hidden. *His instincts are telling him to stay away from my mother.*

"Emily always did like cats." She sneezed. "We should be going."

"Where are you staying?"

Drew pulled a slip of paper from his pocket. "A place called The Outside Inn. Do you know it?"

"Our good friend Coralee Saunders runs the place. You'll love it there."

"And the food is delicious," added Maddy. "There's a cat café at the inn."

Emily said, "How long are you staying in town?"

"Just a few days, maybe a week. We're trying to get the house ready to sell."

Emily said, "I wish you'd reconsider selling the house. You won't find anything nearly as nice, and the mortgage is paid off."

"It's too big for the two of us. Besides, it's time to begin a new chapter in my life." She squeezed Drew's hand.

"There's an arts festival going on this weekend. Maybe we can go together," said Maddy.

"That would be lovely." Frances sneezed again. "I'll call you when we settle in."

Chapter 2

Henry woke up early the next morning and had a plateful of hot, blueberry pancakes on the table when Emily got out of the shower.

"How was your run?" said Henry.

"It gave me a chance to think. I can't believe my sister could still be alive. I think Mom's grasping at straws." She poured herself some coffee and filled Chester's water bowl.

"Without talking to this person who supposedly saw her, or having DNA evidence, it's nothing more than speculation. What are the odds of two kidnappings that far apart?"

"I know. The odds are so slim. I wonder if she called my father?"

"Isn't he still working over in Asia?"

"Yes, but he has a phone."

Maddy came into the kitchen cradling Chester. "Who doesn't have a phone these days?"

Henry said, "No one. It's a law. Everyone has to have a cell phone or they go to jail."

Maddy rolled her eyes and grabbed a plate.

"There are plenty of pancakes. Help yourself. Mom was wondering if her father was aware of the new development."

"I can check social media and see if anyone's heard about this kidnapping. If so, I'll bet we can find the name of that woman who escaped. Maybe Detective Megan will have some ideas."

Emily said, "We have to meet Megan at the bridal store at ten to pick out bridesmaid dresses."

"That'll be fun. She said she'd show us her dress while we're there."

Henry said, "She's already got a dress?"

"I think she's had it picked out for a while. She was just waiting on your buddy Pat to pop the question," said Emily. "They've already started checking out venues."

"Pat's walking on air. I'm really happy for him," said Henry. "Any ideas for plans with Frances and Drew today?"

"I was thinking we could meet them for lunch at Coralee's, then head over to the fair. It was nice out when I ran this morning. Looks like it's going to be a warm winter day." She speared a pancake off the top of the stack.

"Jessica and Sam are going there today," said Maddy. "It's funny, my half-sister found me, and now you're going to find your sister."

"Hopefully," said Emily. "It's a lot to wrap my head around."

"What's your sister like?"

"She was really—I know this sounds trite but I can't think of a better word—sweet. Always trying to please us, but got frustrated when she couldn't do simple things like tie her own shoes. I read to her a lot. She loved stories. Loved to hear the same stories over and over again. And she had the singing voice of an angel."

"I'd love to meet her. Did she like cats?"

"Loved them. Dogs, too. She always said when she grew up she was going to get a Beagle and name him Snoopy. My mother wouldn't allow pets."

"If you find her, we can bring her to the cat café. And she'll love Prancer, right? She can go for walks with him and Kurt."

Henry said, "Let's not get ahead of ourselves."

"Henry's right," said Emily. "This could just be wishful thinking on my mother's part. There isn't a shred of proof that she's alive. She couldn't swim. I don't see how she'd have made it out of that river."

After breakfast, Emily and Maddy met Megan at the bridal shop downtown. The quaint boutique was nestled between a book store and a candy shop. A bell tinkled when they crossed the threshold and the owner nodded at Megan as if she'd been expecting her.

Maddy said, "I want to see your dress!"

"Mine's on order, but come, look at the sample." Megan combed through the rack and held up a strapless, white, satin fit and flare. "I fell in love with this dress the moment I tried it on. My mother was here last weekend. She was beginning to think her over-the-hill detective daughter was never going to get married."

"Thirty-six is hardly over the hill," said Emily. It once sounded old to her, but now that she was in her fifties...

"Do you have a veil?" asked Maddy.

"Yes, it's over here." She pulled down a veil with a beaded headband and pearls sewn into the netting, then slipped it on her head.

Emily said, "It's stunning. What a beautiful bride you'll be." Someday she might help Maddy pick out her own wedding dress—after medical school, or her appointment to the Supreme Court, that is. Although Maddy was more of a jeans and t-shirt kind of girl, Emily couldn't help but notice how her eyes lit up when Megan twirled in front of the mirror in her gown.

Megan said, "I want to go with blue for the bridesmaid dresses. It'll match everyone's coloring. My other bridesmaid is blonde and fair like Maddy. Too bad she had to work today. I was thinking tea length since we're planning a late afternoon wedding. Or do you think floor length is preferable?"

Emily rarely saw this feminine side of Megan, a serious, hard-working detective who had risen quickly up the ranks. "Did the two of you pick a date yet?"

"Late spring or early summer, depending on the availability of venues. I suppose June is pretty popular."

"Around here, fall is the favored season. It's so pretty with the leaves changing colors and all."

Megan held up two dresses. "What do you think of these?" Megan's diamond engagement ring sparkled under the soft boutique lights.

"It's pretty," said Maddy.

Emily imagined it would hang nicely, not too clingy, not too prom-like. "I like it, too."

"Why don't you try them on?" Megan had the owner prepare two dressing rooms.

While changing, Emily said, "I had an interesting visit with my mother yesterday. She thinks my sister, who drowned thirty years ago, may still be alive."

"You're kidding. What brought that on?"

"Back in New York, a woman was kidnapped but managed to escape her captor. She claims the kidnapper wasn't alone. There was a woman there who had Down's syndrome and was in her forties. That could describe my sister, Amy."

"And many others," said Megan.

"The woman has the same color hair as Amy, and a scar on her hand, like my sister had."

"Then, what are you waiting for? Has your mother already met her?"

"No. The kidnapper and this woman are on the lam. By the time the police found the cabin, they were long gone."

"There have been cases, though not a lot, of missing persons turning up years later, alive and well. It's unusual for a kidnapper to abduct two girls so many years apart."

Maddy stepped out of the dressing room. "What do you think?" She rotated, watching herself in the three-way mirror, smile shining through her eyes.

"I love it," said Megan. "Emily, do you have yours on yet?"

Emily stepped out and gave a twirl. "Ta da."

"We can keep looking, but I have to tell you, I love this one."

"And we can wear it again," said Emily, though she knew it wasn't true. She wished she had a nickel for every bride that suggested it. It was intended to make shelling out the money a little easier to swallow, she supposed. Maddy snapped a selfie in the mirror.

"It's a go." Megan clapped her hands together.

The owner came over toting a tape measure and order form. "Let's go ahead and write this up."

Emily discreetly glanced at the price tag. She had to admit, as far as bridesmaid dresses went, it wasn't overly extravagant. She'd just gotten an advance from her publisher that would cover the cost.

"Megan, we're meeting my mother and her new husband at the inn for lunch. Do you and Pat want to join us?"

"Pat's at the hospital this morning working. We're going to meet up later and go to the arts fair."

"So are we. We'll see you there."

Maddy said, "Should I wear my hair up or down?"

Emily said, "We can talk to my hair stylist. Maybe she can give us both up dos." Her own hair was probably too short but her stylist was awfully creative.

I've never been in a wedding before."

"It'll be great," said Megan. "I'd call this a successful morning. I'll see you later."

By the time they'd finished, it was nearly time for lunch. They swung by home to pick up Henry, then headed to the inn.

The Sugarbury Outside Inn looked like a picture from, no, rather the cover of, a tourism brochure. The yellow, wooden inn with the white trim and wrap-around porch stood on a small hill with a golf course adjacent to the dining room. With floor to ceiling windows in the dining room, the view changed with the season, from the lush green golf course of summer, to brilliant colored fall foliage, to a blanket of white punctuated with icy, snow-dusted trees. They walked up the porch past the wicker rockers and Adirondack chairs. Coralee, huggable as a marshmallow, greeted them in the lobby.

"Emily, your parents are just lovely. I'm surprised I haven't seen them here before." She wiped her pudgy hands on her apron.

"It's complicated. Drew's not my real father and they travel a lot."

"Well, they are waiting for you. I gave you the corner table by the window. Maddy, I've got a grilled veggie sandwich and those sweet potato fries you like on the menu today."

When they walked into the dining room, Emily's parents stood up. Her mother said, "This place is a little gem. The owner is a doll."

"She's a good friend and she works hard running the inn."

"Did you talk to your friend in Westbrook? The one whose daughter is a detective?" Her mother spread the linen napkin on her lap.

"Mom, I just found this out last night. I haven't yet had a chance."

Maddy said, "But we were trying on dresses with Detective Megan this morning and she says she's seen cases where missing persons turn up after a lot of years."

Emily said, "Megan said it was possible but not usual. Let's not get our hopes up."

Maddy said, "I found my sister after fourteen years. Well, she found me. Actually, she's my half-sister."

Frances sat up straight. "Really?"

"She found me through one of those DNA kits. We have the same father."

Henry corrected her. "You have the same sperm donor."

"Whatever. Anyhow, he's in jail. Long story."

"What are the odds? See, anything is possible. Do you see her often?"

"She moved to Sugarbury Falls and she teaches school. Her boyfriend is a teacher too."

Emily picked up the menu. "All the dishes are good. Maddy and I don't eat meat. I can tell you the salads are terrific, and Coralee said there's a grilled veggie sandwich today."

Henry said, "But if you really want a treat…"

"And don't care about eating carcasses," added Maddy.

"The burgers are thick as catchers' mitts and juicy as anything."

"You've convinced me," said Drew. "And sounds like a nice cold beer would be a good complement to it."

The waitress took their orders and brought out drinks.

Henry said, "Drew, are you retired?"

"I took early retirement from the army, then worked in technology. Private sector paid better, but I got my full military benefits. It was a win-win. I've been fully retired going on five years now."

"Have you been married before?" asked Emily. Frances shot her a look.

"Yes. Married and divorced."

The reporter in her couldn't resist. "Just once?"

Frances gave her a sharper look, the lines around her mouth stretching into the corners of her lips. Emily enjoyed turning the tables by making her mother uncomfortable.

"Once. Didn't expect to get a second chance, but then I found your mother." He put his arm around Frances.

Emily said, "Do you have children?"

"I've got a son in his thirties. He lives out in California."

"Emily, stop grilling him," said Frances. "This isn't an interview for one of your news reports." Her mother kept forgetting she'd retired from her job as a journalist when they moved to Vermont. She had just opened her mouth to reply when Henry said to Drew, "Army, huh? Did you see any action?"

Drew answered, "I paid my dues. Two years in Vietnam. Two years I'd never want to relive. Lucky you were young enough to have missed it." *I guess he's older than I thought.*

"I had a patient about your age who came in last month with severe PTSD. He was a Vietnam War vet. Told me some stories. He'd been on medication for decades but had stopped taking it."

"Was he okay?"

"Yeah. We got him back on track. He lived with his daughter but she'd gone out of town and without her oversight he'd forgotten to take his pills."

"Food's here. Doesn't that look delicious?" said Frances. "I haven't had an old fashioned potpie in years."

After a good period of silence while the food took center stage, Emily said, "I think you'll enjoy the arts festival. It's more of an arts and crafts fair, not one of those high-brow juried events. It's on the grounds of St. Edwards where I teach. Looks like the weather is cooperating."

"You're teaching college now?"

"Yes, Mom." She'd only told her half a dozen times that she'd taken a part-time position on the faculty.

Henry said, "Last year it was pouring down rain. They moved everything inside."

"Will they ship paintings, if we see something we like? We'll have lots of new walls to fill. I sorted through and got rid of a lot of what we had."

"Why?" said Emily. "You had some lovely paintings. I hope you kept the hand-made rugs from our trip to the South West."

Frances didn't answer. Instead, she said, "Time to move on and start fresh. Is that a dessert cart?" Coralee pushed the cranky cart through the dining room.

Maddy said, "Last year they had funnel cakes and home-made ice cream at the fair. You might want to wait for dessert."

Henry paid the check. "Onward. We can all squeeze into Emily's Audi if you don't mind. Or you can follow us."

"We can go together. It'll give us more time to chat," said Emily's mother. Maddy glared at Emily, like it was her fault she'd be squeezed in the backseat with Frances and Drew. *It was Henry who'd suggested riding together.*

Emily caught a glimpse of her mother and Drew in the rear view mirror, poor Maddy squished between them, trying her best not to touch shoulders with either of them. She could have offered to let Drew with his long legs sit in the front, but she opted not to. It wasn't far to St. Edwards. They rode past snow covered pines, storybook farms with red barns and silos, and an authentic dry goods store. When Henry turned onto a curvy mountain road, the small college campus came into view.

Frances's eyes were glued to the window. "Is that where you work? It looks like a medieval village."

"Yes. My office is in there." She pointed to a moss-covered stone building. She was thankful for her faculty parking pass. Had she not had access to the lot outside her office, they'd have had a long walk ahead of them. Not usually a problem, but stuffed with Coralee's food it would have been a challenge. She briefly thought about showing her mother her office but decided against it.

"Onward," said Henry. As they got closer, he said, "I smell funnel cakes and hot, roasted cashews." They passed a food tent and a cotton candy machine just past the entrance.

Frances said, "There are rows and rows of vendors. When you said arts fair, I hadn't imagined it being so expansive."

"It's a big deal. There's even a literature contest. One of my students won last year," said Emily.

Frances ran her fingers over a macramé rug. "I read one of your books over the Christmas holiday. We were on a cruise and the television choices were slim to say the least."

She had to ask, though she knew better. "What did you think?"

"It was a little dark, wouldn't you say?"

"It's true crime, not a cozy mystery. It's hard to write realistically about a kidnapping or a murdered child without being dark." She imagined Henry's voice inside her head telling her not to get defensive.

"There's a woman in my yoga class who writes books." She said it nonchalantly, as if she were telling her about a friend who baked cookies or knit sweaters. "Look, pottery!"

"Emily, over here." She spun around. Her neighbor, Abby, motioned her over. She stood in front of a display of photographs.

Emily pointed to the display. "Abby, those are exquisite. You really captured the essence of Lake Pleasant."

"They've been selling well. I brought along some black and white wedding photos I took last week. My photography business is filling my schedule nicely but I'll take every chance to advertise."

"You should talk to Megan O'Leary. I doubt she's lined up a photographer for her wedding yet. She and Pat said they were coming this afternoon. Where's your lovely wife?"

"Rebecca is working on her Christmas list. You know how much of a planner she is."

Frances and Drew came over. "Abby, this is my Mom, Frances, and her husband, Drew. She and her wife live a few cabins down from us."

A customer asked Abby for help. "Excuse me."

Frances whispered to Emily. "Did she say her wife? I mean, I know it's getting to where it's legal some places but she didn't even blink an eye."

"Why should she?" Emily looked straight into her eyes, holding the gaze, while Frances squirmed.

Frances turned and quickly thumbed through the framed photographs on the table. "Drew, these would look lovely in the hallway. Which ones do you like?"

Henry said, "Where'd Maddy go?"

"She said she saw Jessica around the corner. Come on. Mom, we'll be in the next aisle."

They worked their way through kids holding balloons, parents holding caramel-coated hands, and a woman pushing a Yorkie in a pink stroller.

"Dr. Fox? Is that you?"

"Hey, how's the broken wrist doing?"

While Henry chatted with his patient, Emily sat on a bench in front of a leafless oak tree and bent down to tie her sneaker. She heard arguing behind her.

"You will not get away with what you did. The court may have let you off but not me."

"It wasn't my fault. Leave me alone." The man had a bit of a lisp, making him seem younger, more vulnerable.

"And now what? You're gonna go right back and do it again? Over my dead body." This was rage speaking. Emily was scared he might turn violent and reached for her phone. Should she call the police?

"You're an ass." It came out sounding, like, 'you're an asp,' but Emily knew what he meant.

"Own up to it. It's your last chance. I've waited long enough for an admission of guilt and an apology. Today's the day."

"You can wait till hell freezes over. Get out of my face."

Emily was afraid to move. It was a few moments before she'd convinced herself the men had left and she felt comfortable getting up. She worked her way back to where she'd left Henry. Henry had wandered off, lured by a display of wood furniture under a canopy they'd passed.

"Henry, I'm glad I found you." She was out of breath.

"Emily, what's wrong?"

"Nothing. Two guys were arguing, I thought a fight was about to break out, but they stopped. See anything good?"

"That bookshelf is nice, but I can make one myself. Don't need to spend the money."

"Look. Popcorn. Let's get some."

"I thought we were going to get dessert."

"Yeah. After the popcorn."

They munched as they browsed through the displays. Emily bought a set of crocheted potholders with roosters on them, excited that they matched their kitchen clock. When they turned the corner, they spotted Maddy with her half-sister and her boyfriend.

Emily said, "Jessica, looks like you've already done a good bit of shopping."

"This is my first time experiencing this extravaganza. Good thing Sam's here to help with the overflow." She nodded at her on-again off-again boyfriend. He wore a stained sweat shirt and dirty running shoes.

"As long as I'm not paying for it, I don't mind schlepping. This is huge. I even saw a table selling used computer parts. What a racket."

Jessica said, "Those were mobiles made from computer parts."

"Maybe that's what I should do with my old hardware. Throw garbage together and call it art. It's tough not getting paid all summer. The life of a teacher."

Jessica said, "That's why you have to budget."

"Look who's talking. You've probably spent half a paycheck on all this...stuff. I'm going to take these out to the car."

When he was out of earshot, Emily said, "He's a real joy to be around. Maddy said you'd broken up."

Maddy said, "The last time I talked to Jessica, that's what she told me." She turned to Jessica, "Right?"

Jessica said, "I know, I know. I keep getting sucked back in. He can be a real charmer when he wants to."

Maddy said, "He's an old geezer. If he complains about his salary, why didn't he keep his old job?"

"He said he wanted to do something more meaningful than fiddling with computers all day long. He's not working that hard as a teacher. It's not like he has the same kids all day and teaches all the subjects like I do. They rotate into his technology class for half an hour at a time and he sticks them in front of computer screens. I think he's just lazy."

Maddy said, "I'll bet he got fired and that's why he moved here."

Henry said, "Cut him loose and keep fishing. That's my advice. There's something sneaky about him."

Someone screamed in the distance.

Emily said, "What's that?"

Someone in the crowd shouted, "A man just fell from the roof. Help!" More screams. People rushed toward the sound.

Henry ran behind Emily. By the time he made it around the corner, a crowd had formed and an overweight, sixtyish-year-old man was sprawled on the ground. A woman of about the same age held his bloody face in her hands and implored him to wake up.

"I'm a doctor. Let me through," said Henry.

"It's my husband. Help him."

Henry bent down and felt for a pulse. "He's not breathing. Call 911." He started compressions.

"Wake up, Toby," screamed the wife.

By this time, Maddy and Jessica had made it around the corner. Emily was appalled at the number of bystanders taking videos.

"Henry, do you want your bag?" From the looks of things, she couldn't imagine the man was still alive. How had he fallen off the roof, face up? And why on Earth was he up there?

"He…my…bag…is…in…the…car." He was looking fatigued as he continued pumping.

"Yes, *two, three, four*. Hurry!"

"I hear sirens," said Maddy.

"What's your husband's name?" asked Henry.

"Toby. Toby Cutler. He said he was going to go buy a funnel cake! He's alive, right?"

Sam came around the corner. "I heard an ambulance. What happened?" The siren screamed as it bullied its way through the crowded lawn.

Jessica said, "He fell from the roof. Where were you, anyway? Didn't you hear his wife screaming?"

Henry stopped and checked for a pulse.

The wife shouted. "Keep trying. Don't let him die." She threw herself over her husband's body.

Henry said, "No, be careful. Don't make him move, he may have a spinal cord injury." He couldn't admit to her that her husband was dead. Radiologists seldom had to report that kind of news, which is one of the reasons he'd chosen that specialty.

The EMTs pushed a stretcher through the crowd. "What's the status?"

"See for yourselves," said Henry.

Emily gently nudged the wife off of her husband. "Let the EMTs check."

They bent down next to the body. Within minutes they confirmed what Henry knew but was reluctant to say. "I'm sorry. There's nothing more we can do."

"What? Aren't you going to keep trying?" His wife sobbed. "Don't let him die. Help him. Wake up, Toby."

Emily placed her hand on the woman's arm. "Come. Can we call someone for you? A family member or a friend?"

"No. My daughter isn't…I'm all alone right now."

"What's your name? I never even asked."

"Lisa."

Emily turned to Henry, "Let's take her home."

"I'm not leaving him. Why aren't they taking him to the hospital?"

Henry said, "They have to wait for the police to come. It's policy. There's nothing more for you to do here. It may take hours." A security guard chased the crowd back.

Jessica said, "Maddy can come home with me."

"Sure. We can drop off Frances and Drew on the way," said Henry.

Megan and Pat pushed through the dissipating crowd.

"Hey, buddy, what happened? Megan got a call on our way over. Someone fell off the roof?"

"You heard right. That's the widow over there." Henry pointed at Lisa.

Megan said, "Were there any witnesses?" She looked at the remaining people and shouted, "Don't go anywhere yet."

"He fell face up. It doesn't make sense," said Henry.

Megan said to the crowd, "Who saw what happened?"

A woman stepped forward. "I heard a scream, then a crash. Then I…He was on the ground…the blood."

"I heard two men arguing right before it happened," said the woman pushing her dog in a stroller. "They were up there." She pointed to the roof.

A man said, "I saw him fall and hit the ground. It was ugly. The other guy ran away."

"What other guy?"

"Either a guy or girl. Couldn't tell. The hoodie was pulled up tight. Ran down the path a few minutes later. Came from there." He pointed at the door. Megan typed into her iPad.

"The back door?"

"Yeah."

"Was he/she tall or short? What color hoodie?"

"I don't know how tall since he was running and all. The hoodie was gray and I think he was wearing jeans."

Emily came over and whispered to Megan. "I called one of Lisa's church friends from her contact list. I told her we'd drive Lisa home."

Lisa said, "I heard you. I don't want to go. Why are the police here?"

Megan said, "We're going to investigate and find out what happened. It's routine. Do you know what he was doing up on the roof?"

"He said he wanted a funnel cake. I have no idea why he was up there."

"Had he been depressed?"

Her face tightened. "You think he did this to himself? That's crazy. Of course not. We're expecting a grandchild. He was over the moon."

"Do you know who he might have been with? Did anyone call before this happened? Did he see a friend while you were together here?"

"Wait. He got a text right before. Stuck the phone back in his pocket."

"Any idea from who?"

"No, he didn't say. I want him off the ground!"

"It's going to be a while. We'll take care of him."

Drew tapped Henry on the shoulder. "Frances wants to know if this means the fair is over. She wanted to buy those photographs."

"Yes, it's over. We'll drop you off at the inn. Come on."

"Come on, Lisa. There's nothing for you to do here." Emily put her arm around Lisa and led her to the car.

When they got to the house, Emily grabbed the mail from the box next to the door, then found the kitchen and put on the tea kettle. Henry got Lisa settled in the living room.

Lisa leafed through the mail. "Oh, no. I can't deal with this now." She threw an envelope on the floor.

"Leave it. Whatever's in the mail can wait," said Henry.

"It's about the lawsuit."

"What lawsuit? If the college was at fault…"

"No, Toby's lawsuit. Toby slipped on the steps of the post office."

"I'm confused. Who's doing the suing?"

"Toby is suing the city. Was suing the city. Also was suing the guy who was responsible for clearing it. It was icy and…he broke his wrist, needed stitches…"

"Don't even think about that now." He picked the letter up off the floor and put it on the desk.

Emily came in with a cup of tea. "Your friend Vicky will be here soon. She's going to stay with you tonight."

"I have to call my daughter. How can I tell her that her father is dead?"

The knock at the door caused Lisa to spill a bit of her tea.

"It must be your friend. I'll let her in."

"Thank you, both. I don't think I'd have found my way back without your help."

"Let us know if you need anything," said Emily.

Chapter 3

The next morning, Emily went out for a run.

What was Toby doing up on that roof? If he wanted a view of the campus, there were better places. Maybe he did try to kill himself. By jumping off the roof on a college campus in the middle of an art fair? No, that was ridiculous. Besides, she heard the woman with the doggie stroller say she heard arguing coming from the roof. Could it have been the same two men who were arguing when I stopped to tie my shoe?

Her gruff Minnesota neighbor approached. "You're up early for a Sunday," said flannel-clad Kurt Olav. He commanded Prancer to sit and the chocolate lab immediately responded.

Emily stopped and wiped her face with the bottom of her running shirt. "I didn't see you coming." She scratched Prancer's head between the ears.

"Did you hear the news last night? Toby Cutler, dead. I can't believe it."

"You knew him?"

"Yeah. I'd seen him around."

"I brought his widow home after it happened. There were still boxes in the dining room. I guess they were new to town."

"They moved here at the end of last summer or so. Said he was sick of the heat. I've been outta Minnesota for years and I've still got a few boxes in the barn."

"What do you know about him?"

"He'd just retired. He was a security guard or something like that. Has a wife and kid around Chloe's age. Hangs out at Ralph's—plays pool."

"I can't figure out what he was doing on the roof. First thought was suicide."

"Nah, can't imagine it. He was living the life. Fishing, hunting...he was even expecting a grandkid. Bought everyone at Ralph's a beer the night he heard."

"He liked hunting? That means he owned a gun."

"Good point. He struck me as a guy who if he did want to end it all would've put a bullet in his head before jumping off a roof." Prancer stood up and gave a single bark as if asking permission to move on.

"Okay, boy. We're going."

"Have a nice walk. You'll have to stop by and meet my mother one of these days."

"I'll do that."

When Emily got back home, Henry was pouring coffee into a thermos.

"I thought you weren't working today?"

"Pat called. He's working on Toby's autopsy and had a few questions. Told him I'd run over there. There's more coffee, and I already fed Chester."

She poured a cup of coffee, then went to take a shower. Although Lisa's friend had stayed with her last night, she thought she'd stop by later in the morning to check on her. She couldn't imagine how poor Lisa must be feeling and hoped the daughter would be able to be with her soon.

Emily's phone rang. "Mom? No, I haven't called her yet. Things were a little crazy yesterday if you remember. Okay, I'll call Susan."

Frankly, she hadn't thought about her sister since the accident yesterday, which surprised her since she'd thought about her sister practically every day for the past thirty years. If the case was out of Westbrook's jurisdiction, she doubted Lynette could do much. On the other hand, if anyone could talk someone into doing something, it was Lynette's headstrong mother, Susan Wiles. If she could only talk to that woman who was kidnapped...She punched in Susan's number.

"Emily? What a nice surprise."

"Good to hear your voice. I miss you and Mike."

"Same here. How's life with a teenager going?"

"It's going. Maddy has adjusted really well, I'd say. You promised you'd come visit this summer. We're still on, right?"

"Yes, we're on. Of course, it'll have to be around wedding plans."

"Whose wedding?"

"Didn't I tell you? Evan finally popped the question. He and Kara are getting married."

"Congratulations!"

"Yeah, it's about time."

"You know, Maddy and I are going to be in a wedding. Megan O'Leary, our police detective, is marrying a close friend of ours. Maddy and I are bridesmaids. How's Mike? How's Lynette?"

"Busy. The girls can be a handful. Mia's walking now and getting into everything."

"Susan, I was wondering if I can ask a favor."

"Of course. What is it?"

"My mother's got this crazy idea in her head. Listen. A girl was kidnapped near Westbrook but escaped. You may have heard the story. The girl saw someone else in the kidnapper's home—a woman with Down's syndrome."

"Yeah, it was all over the news. They interviewed the girl all in shadows. I guess she could still be in danger. They haven't yet caught the guy."

"My mom thinks the woman at the house with the kidnapper was my sister."

"Amy? Is that even possible? Didn't she drown?"

"That's what we all thought, and it's probably the truth only…"

"You have to be sure."

"I know. I was hoping Lynette might help us out. If we could only talk to the woman, maybe we'd know if it was really Amy she saw. The Westbrook police won't investigate because it's not their jurisdiction. If they'd just find the house and run a DNA test on items left behind…"

"You know how Lynette is. She plays by the rules, but I'll work on her."

"Thanks, Susan. I knew I could count on you."

"Don't thank me yet. I'll call you after I talk to her. Imagine if your sister is alive after all these years? By the way, you'll be getting a *Save the Date* magnet in the mail any day now."

"Send Evan my best and kiss Annalise and Mia for me." She put the phone down. She missed Susan and Mike. When they'd all lived in the same town, they had regular card nights, dinners…they were like family.

Emily wondered how the police were coming along with their investigation. She'd like to tell Lisa when the body would be released so she could start thinking about the funeral arrangements. She picked up the phone.

"Megan? It's Emily. Quite an afternoon yesterday. Do you have an idea when Toby Cutler's body will be released? I'm about to head over to Lisa Cutler's place."

"Pat's doing the autopsy this morning. There are some things that don't add up. I'm not ready to close the investigation."

"You don't think it was an accident?"

"No. We found his phone up on the roof. He'd received a text luring him up there. Then there was a witness who saw someone running away from the building."

"When I dropped Lisa Cutler off yesterday, there was a piece of mail that upset her. Something about Toby suing the city."

"I'll look into it. I've got some work to do before I'm satisfied so I can't yet tell her when the body will be released. Pat's still working on the autopsy, like I said."

"Okay. Well, I'll let you go."

Emily got herself together. Maddy was still asleep, as usual for a weekend. Before stopping at Lisa's, she took a detour to St. Edwards. She wasn't sure what she was looking for, but had an urge to look over the area. The arts fair which was scheduled to run through the weekend had been postponed in light of yesterday's events. She parked behind her office and walked over to the building from which Toby had fallen.

The building was only three stories high, like most of the others on campus. A handwritten sign said 'restrooms' and pointed toward the door. That meant there were lots of fair goers in and out of the building. No one going in would have stuck out as odd. Toby had fallen onto the stone path, still marked off with yellow tape and a chalk outline. Emily tried the door. Open. She climbed the stairs leading to the roof and pushed open the door.

The view wasn't particularly spectacular. It was the closest building to where the fair had been set up. A trail along the edge of the woods curved around the side. That's most likely how whoever was with Toby had escaped. Or he could have simply exited right through the main door and blended in with others using the restrooms.

The roof was littered with cigarette butts. There was a yellow evidence marker next to an average size shoeprint and another next to what could be a drag mark. She assumed it marked where he was when he fell or was pushed. It hadn't rained in days. Why the muddy print?

She went back down the stairs and out the back door. *Turning right, the killer would have run along the path and easily could have run into the woods to escape.* She set out on the path, head down, looking for more shoeprints or any other clue as she trudged through the snowy mud. Nothing.

Chapter 4

   While Emily explored the accident scene, Henry met Pat at the morgue.

   "Pat, what's up? Megan push you to get here at the crack of dawn to do this autopsy?"

   "I'm hoping to wrap this up and spend the afternoon looking at wedding venues with her."

   "You're hoping to be dragged in and out of country clubs and churches?"

   "I'm in love. What can I tell you?"

   "Picking out a honeymoon venue sounds like more fun. You haven't taken vacation time since I've known you."

   "I will be now. I've been looking at all sorts of warm destinations. The Caribbean, Bermuda, maybe even Hawaii if Megan can get the time off."

   "What's the difference? You'll be spending most of your time in your room if you know what I mean. I'm happy for you, buddy. Let's hurry and get you out of here. What did you find?"

   "To start with, no defensive wounds. If he'd struggled with someone, I'd see some evidence of it. He fell backwards. Generally, a suicide victim goes to the edge and plunges off. Also, there was a receipt in his pocket. Looks like he'd just bought some hand-made furniture at the arts fair less than an hour before he went up to the roof. Why do that if you were about to jump?"

   "Okay, so it's not a suicide and there wasn't a struggle. Was it an accident?"

"When I opened him up, I found this." He showed Henry a small piece of machinery. "It's not a pacemaker."

Henry looked. "No, it's called an ICD, an internal defibrillator. Same idea as a pace maker. Gives the heart a shock if it goes out of rhythm."

"Could it have malfunctioned?"

"I doubt it. These things are built to do the job." Pat examined the device. "This is really mangled. I can't read the serial number."

"Let me see. The newer devices are monitored remotely. If we can trace this back to his doctor, he might have a record of Toby's heart activity." He held it up to his eye. "I can't read it."

Pat put it under his microscope. "I can't make out the numbers. I'll see if Megan can send it to the crime lab."

"Of course, we may be able to get his health information from his widow."

"You can ask. I'll get this written up and talk to Megan."

"I hate bothering our victim's wife at a time like this. She was a mess yesterday."

"I understand. I know how it felt when my wife died. For the longest time I'd wake up and have to remind myself she wasn't just in the shower or making coffee. Hope she's got some support."

"She has a daughter and one of her church friends was there with her last night. Knowing Emily, she'll be bringing over food and keeping an eye on her."

"Let me know if you find his doctor. I'm sure the family wants to know what happened."

"All right. Have fun at your venues." He wondered if Emily was still over at Toby's house. When he got to the Jeep, he called her.

"Em, it's me. I just finished talking to Pat. He completed the autopsy. I'm trying to find out the name of Toby's cardiologist. Can you ask his wife about it?"

"Cardiologist? You think he had a heart attack up there?"

"I just need to check some information."

"Sure." He heard her question the widow. "She says she doesn't remember. It was implanted back in Florida. He had a history of heart issues and he'd been like a new man since he had the device put in."

"Doesn't remember his doctor's name?"

"No. She's got a lot on her mind."

"How about which hospital he went to?"

"Henry, can it wait?"

"I guess so." After hanging up, he made his way to the emergency department. He checked the cubicles. "No patients? As in zero?"

A nurse answered. "That's right. And Dr. Edwards is coming in in an hour. You should take advantage of the opportunity. For being semi-retired, you work too hard."

"You're right." He checked his phone messages, then gathered his things and drove home.

When he got home, Maddy was in the living room, talking on the phone. When she realized he was home early, she said, "I love you" and she stuck the phone in the pocket of her jeans.

"Who were you talking to?"

"No one. Why are you home so early?"''

"Maddy, I heard you tell someone you loved them. Who was it?"

"Mind your own business."

"Don't you dare talk to me like that. I'm your father and it's my job to protect you. Are you seeing someone?"

"So what if I am. I'm almost fifteen."

"Understood, but you're living under my roof. Why are you keeping it a secret? You think I won't approve of him? You're probably right."

"I can't say."

"Then give me your phone. You can have it back when you show some respect and stop keeping secrets." He reached for her pocket and she pulled back.

"Give it to me."

"Okay, okay. It's not a boyfriend. I was talking to my father."

Henry felt his stomach somersault. "What do you mean? He's in jail. We told you to stay away from him when we caught you with his letters."

"I have a right to know my own father. Besides, he's educated and a good man. He shouldn't be in prison."

"Are you crazy? He was misleading all those patients, including your mother. It's unforgiveable what he did."

"He was trying to make them happy. He only used his sperm for the patients who couldn't find an appropriate match. Who did it harm?"

"You, for one."

"Why? I knew nothing about the anonymous donor. Now I know my father was a doctor and a humanitarian. And I have his eyes. See." She showed him a picture on her phone."

He felt his blood boil. "He's sending you pictures! Maddy, this has to stop. I'm going to call the prison and make sure he has no further contact with you."

"You're just jealous because he's my real father."

"Is he putting a roof over your head and food in your stomach? Did he help you build a cat café and create kick butt science fair projects? This isn't jealousy; it's concern."

"If you stop me, I'll just run to him the minute I turn eighteen anyway."

"By then maybe you'll be mature enough to understand. Even your sister said to stay away back when she found out he was writing to you."

"She's not me. And don't go telling Emily. She'll freak out even more than you are. I thought you'd be the understanding one." She stormed off. Henry braced himself…there it was…the door slam.

"Your mother must be turning over in her grave." Did he really just sound like his own grandmother? How could Maddy fall for this nonsense? She told him she loved him! She'd never even said that to him or Emily and she was saying it to this convict father she hadn't even met. He heard Emily's car in the driveway. His first instinct was to spill the whole encounter he'd just had with Maddy, but with all the drama involving Amy on her mind right now it might be better to spare Emily for the time being.

Emily tossed her keys on the hall table. "What's wrong? You look upset."

"Nothing. Just, um, thinking about what happened at the fair. How's the widow holding up?"

"You can only imagine. Her pregnant daughter's arriving today. On top of losing her husband, Lisa's worried about how the news might affect the baby."

"Babies are resilient, even before birth."

"Yes, but you can understand how she'd be worried. What happened with the autopsy?"

"Pat didn't find evidence of a struggle. He discovered the guy had an implantable heart device, sort of like a pacemaker."

"That's why you asked about his cardiologist. You think Toby had a heart attack and fell off the roof?"

"The device is meant to prevent a heart attack and they are extremely effective. Anyhow, yes, that's why I asked about his doctor. It's possible he has the data from the device and that can tell us a lot."

"How would he have data?"

"It's called remote monitoring. Pretty remarkable really. With the right software, the doctor can see the heart rhythm in real time."

"Maybe the daughter will know. I'm sure she can at least tell us the name of the hospital. She must have visited while he was in there."

"It would have been a short hospital stay. If she doesn't live in town, she may not."

"Is Maddy home?"

"She's in her room."

"I'll go say hello."

"I wouldn't. She's in one of her moods."

"About what? She was fine last night."

"Who knows. She mumbled something about friends." He hated lying to Emily.

"I stopped by the college and went up to the roof, just to see."

"And?"

"I found a muddy shoe print and cigarette butts. Police had already placed evidence markers. The building was open to the public for restroom access. Anyone could have gone up there unnoticed."

"I though a witness identified someone running away. And someone told Megan she heard arguing up on the roof shortly before Toby fell."

"Like I said, there was open access to the building. Even if someone appeared to be fleeing the scene, it isn't a certainty that's who was on the roof. But..."

"But what?"

"While you were talking to that patient at the arts fair, I heard two men arguing when I stopped to tie my shoe. One was clearly threatening the other. I wish I'd gotten a look at them."

"You don't know who they were, so don't stress over it. The police will get this. I was going to make a sandwich. Want one?"

"Sure. There's a new jar of almond butter in the pantry."

"Pat and Megan are going to look at venues this afternoon. He sounded excited. Who'd have figured."

"Things seem to be moving along. She has the dresses picked out and once they find a venue, they can set the date. I talked to Susan. Evan and Kara are finally engaged."

"She's been waiting for that, hasn't she? Good for them. Two doctors ought to have a good lifestyle. I can't imagine messing it up."

"Messing it up? What are you talking about?"

He couldn't help wondering how Maddy's father wound up risking his medical career for the ego boost of fathering all those kids. "Nothing. Let's eat. I'm starving."

Chapter 5

Emily thought the buzzing phone was part of a dream before fully wakening. She turned over and reached for the nightstand. "Mom, I just woke up. The police won't tell you what?"

"The kidnapper took his victim to Watuga but the Watuga police won't give me any information as to what areas they searched. If they find the cabin, I'm sure there's enough DNA somewhere left for them to trace. As a matter of fact, I'll go myself. As a matter of fact, I'm going to pack and go."

"No, Mom. It's like literally trying to find a needle in a haystack. Susan's daughter might look into it for us so hold your horses, okay?"

"Can she find out about the victim? If only we could talk to her."

"I'll touch base with Susan later. Hang on. We can't go every which way with this or we'll never zero in on the truth. I'll get back to you. Go have breakfast."

Henry came out of the shower. "Was that your mother at this hour?"

"Yes. She was about to drive to Watuga and start going door to door. I talked her out of it."

"Good. You going running?"

She pulled the curtains aside, half-hoping for rain so she'd have an excuse to skip it. Instead, she saw an orange sun rising over the mountain. "Yeah. Then I need to get working on my book."

"I'll be at the hospital. Are you going to check on the widow?"

"Sometime later."

"If her daughter is there, can you ask her if she knows the name of her father's cardiologist or the hospital where he had his surgery?"

"Sure." She pulled on her running socks and laced her trainers. "Let's eat dinner at the inn tonight. This way I can make sure my mom doesn't skip town." She gave him a kiss.

After she left, Henry knocked on Maddy's door. "I want to talk to you before you leave for school. I'll be in the kitchen. Want some scrambled eggs?" She didn't answer. "Suit yourself."

He started the coffee and took the eggs out of the fridge. He retrieved the paper and as soon as he unrolled it, the front page picture of Toby Cutler and the headline, *Security Guard Tumbles to his Death* stared back at him.

He skimmed through the story. Toby Cutler was ex-military. He'd moved here with his wife last fall, and he'd just been hired as a part-time security guard for the school system. Henry guessed he needed the money, or that he'd become bored with retirement, like he had, and looked for part-time work. Survived by a daughter and wife... the incident is under investigation by the Sugarbury Falls police.

Maddy slammed her backpack onto the counter and filled Chester's bowl, splashing water all over the floor.

Henry made her a plate of eggs. He knew the best course of action would be to ignore her childish behavior. "Breakfast." He sat down at the table with her.

"Did you blab to Emily about my phone call?"

"First of all, you will not speak to me disrespectfully, whether you're angry or not. Secondly, there are no secrets between Emily and me." He wouldn't let her have the satisfaction of thinking he'd kept it to himself, even though he had.

"Why don't you come with me then? We fly into Chicago and visit together."

"Maddy, it's not a good idea. Think about the people he's hurt, not to mention his disregard for the law and his professional ethics."

"If you don't…"

"Don't go making threats. And this isn't the time to be stressing Emily out. She's dealing with enough in light of the news Amy may be alive."

Maddy grumbled. She ate a few bites, then dumped the plate into the garbage disposal.

Henry called to her as she stormed out of the kitchen. "Love you. Have a sunshiny good day." Then he picked up his phone to call Maddy's sister.

"Jessica, are you teaching yet?"

"I'm just getting my classroom set up. Is Maddy okay?"

"I heard her talking to your father last night. That's right…at the prison."

"I thought we'd talked her out of making contact when she was getting letters from him."

"Apparently not. I don't know what to do."

"What's Emily think?"

"I didn't want to tell her since she's dealing with her own problems and also keeping an eye on Lisa Cutler, the wife of the guy who fell off the roof yesterday."

"Can you call the prison and have them block his calls?"

"I don't know. I'll try that. Meanwhile, can you try to talk some sense into her?"

"Of course, but Maddy is pretty stubborn."

"She even suggested us taking her to visit the prison."

"That's no place for her. How could she want to meet that creep anyway? I'll talk to her."

"Thanks, Jessica."

He took out his laptop and googled the name of the prison where Maddy's father resided. Then he called the prison and asked to speak to the warden.

"Don't put me on hold!" What choice did he have?

His patience waning, he was about to hang up, when he heard a voice on the other end.

"This is Warden Thompson."

"My name is Dr. Henry Fox. I want to prohibit one of your prisoner's from calling my daughter. What's the procedure?"

"Is this inmate harassing your daughter?"

"Not really."

"Mr. Fox, prisoners have access to the phone in the evenings. Without a court order, we can't stop them from making a call."

"My daughter is legally a minor."

"The easiest way to deal with the situation would be for you to simply block the number on your end. Prisoners are not permitted to receive calls."

"Thank you."

Why hadn't he thought of that? Simply block the number. But Maddy could unblock it if he did it from her phone. He called the phone company and found out what to do. Apps to control your child's access to phone numbers as well as games and web sites? Who knew? He'd learned so much in the short amount of time he'd been a father. He looked at his watch and hustled to get ready for work.

***

By the time Emily returned from her run, the house was quiet. She sat down to work on her book, but her thoughts kept drifting. Toby was suing someone. Was it a motive? Possibly. She needed more information. She managed to work a bit, then headed to Lisa Cutler's house.

Lisa's daughter, quite pregnant, answered the door. "Yes?"

"I'm Emily Fox. I told your mom I'd drop by and check on her this morning. I'm so sorry for your loss."

"Shari Townshend. Come on in. She finally fell asleep. She was up most of the night. We both were."

"Let her sleep. You should try to rest, too."

"I can't. Mom's doctor prescribed sleeping pills for her but obviously in my condition I'm on my own. I don't know how this makes sense. Why was my father on the roof in the middle of a fair?"

"The police are working on it."

"Did you know my father well?"

"Honestly, I'd never met him. I was at the fair and stepped in to help your mother get home. My husband is a doctor. He tried to help your father but the injuries were too severe. My husband's friend is the medical examiner who performed the autopsy."

"This really is a small town."

"Do you know the name of your father's cardiologist by any chance? Your mother couldn't remember."

"No. He had the device inserted at our local hospital. St. Anne's in Coral Way, Florida."

"That's helpful."

Do you want some tea or something? There's cake. People from her church dropped by with cakes and casseroles last night."

"She seems to have a good support system."

Lisa, hair a mess, wearing yoga pants and an oversized shirt which Emily guessed was Toby's, Stumbled into the room.

"Mom, sit down. Your friend Emily is here."

"Emily, you didn't have to go out of your way."

"I wanted to see if you needed anything."

"I need to understand how this happened is what I need. I need my husband here with me."

"Henry is trying to get in touch with your husband's doctor. Perhaps he had a heart attack and fell."

"No. He's got that thing in his chest. Someone had to have pushed him. He got that text right before..."

"What text?"

"Someone wanted to talk to him. That's when he went up to the roof."

"Any idea who was texting him?"

"No."

"Can you think of anyone who wanted him dead? You mentioned a law suit."

"Yeah. Toby was suing the guy for every cent he had, plus the city. Said we were going to be rich in the end and we could move to the Bahamas. Pipe dream's what I told him."

Emily felt lost, like she had an outline but needed it colored in. *What was the lawsuit about?* "Do you know the name of the man who he was suing?"

"Charlie something." She shuffled papers on a wooden desk. "Here. It's the whole case summary and contact info. Both lawyers are in there, his and Charlie's."

"Do you mind if I take this? I can drop it off at the police station if you'd like."

"Knock yourself out. If it helps, great."

"Can I do anything for you before I leave?"

"No. Just find us some answers. It won't bring Toby back, but I need to know what really happened up on that roof."

Emily went back home. Before turning over the documents to the police, she wanted to make copies and do her own research. Megan had her hands full these days putting together a wedding and her partner, Detective Ron Wooster, was on vacation.

She opened up her laptop and got to work. Charlie Adams. Narrow it down. Charlie Adams Sugarbury Falls. No luck. He worked for the post office…This was going nowhere. She called Abby's wife, Rebecca, her tech savvy neighbor but she didn't answer the phone.

She'd barely put down the phone when it began vibrating. Susan Wiles. She knew her old friend would come through.

"Susan? Did you talk to Lynette?"

"Yes. She told me the police think they found the cabin where the victim was being held."

"That's great! Were they able to test for fingerprints or DNA?"

"There's a complication."

"What complication? Who has to put in the request? I'm Amy's sister. Who should I talk to at the Watuga police station?"

"It's not that. The cabin they found was burned to the ground. Completely gone. Lynette's friend over in Watuga says it was arson."

"The kidnapper knew the police would be looking once the recent victim escaped and burned it down?"

"Looks that way. I didn't get all the details, but Lynette said it was done by someone who knew what they were doing, whatever that means."

"The kidnapper either worked with fire before, or he's intelligent enough to do research and figure it out. Must have hightailed it outta there quickly once the recent victim escaped."

"You think he was a fire fighter?" asked Susan.

"Not necessarily. Could be a forest ranger or, I don't know. Do they have any leads?"

"Lynette didn't know of any, but they're working on it."

"You'll let me know if you hear anything?"

"Of course. Hang in there, Emily. I'm praying for you to find her."

"Thanks, Susan. Tell Lynette how much I appreciate her help." She digested what Susan told her. Locating the cabin meant they had a starting point for putting out a search. How far could someone get each day in any direction from the cabin? Amy certainly wasn't the athletic type back when she was fourteen. She must be slowing him down. If she could get the exact location of the cabin...

Then again, she needed to trust the professionals. This wasn't a cold case for the Watuga police, it was a recent kidnapping. Surely the victim and her family were pushing them. The victim. She wished she could talk to her. She understood the need to keep her identity a secret but...No. Lynette would never cross that line.

She went back to work researching Charlie Adams but ran into a wall. Feeling frustrated, she hoped a quick walk might help. Maybe she'd even stop by and see if Rebecca was home.

She'd barely begun her walk when she ran into Kurt and Prancer.

"That dog sure keeps you in shape, Kurt." Prancer was no longer a puppy, but he was full of energy. She'd thought about getting a dog to keep her company on her walks and runs but didn't think Chester would be amenable to the idea.

"Hey, Emily. I thought I saw you out running earlier?"

"Yeah. I needed a walk to clear my head. I've got my sister on my mind, and I'm trying to help Lisa Cutler make sense of her husband's death."

"I'm gonna miss him down at Ralph's. All the guys will."

"All the guys?"

"You know, the regulars."

"Did you ever run into a guy named Charlie Adams?"

"Charlie Adams? There's a Charlie who shows up to play pool some nights. Don't know the last name."

"This Charlie works at the post office."

"I don't know. All I know is this Charlie doesn't work nights, and he likes his Budweiser."

"Did Toby know him?"

"Sure. Ralph's is a small place. We all knew each other. We all toasted Toby last night. He'll be missed."

"Did Charlie seem upset about Toby?"

"He wasn't hooping and hollering over the news if that's what you mean. None of us were."

"Thanks. I'm trying to find Charlie Adams because Toby was suing him over an incident at the post office. Chances are he isn't even the same Charlie."

"You gotta picture?"

"No. Not yet anyway."

"If you find one run it by me. Otherwise, you and Henry can stop over and have a drink at Ralph's. See for yourselves."

"I wouldn't know him if I fell over him at this point. Thanks, Kurt. Bye, Prancer."

"Look how Prancer loves you. You should get yourself a dog, Emily. The guy in the cabin next to the one I rent out is expecting puppies any day now. You should talk to him."

"I'd love to, but Chester doesn't take well to other animals. We tried bringing home another cat once and she was miserable."

"It'd be a little puppy, no threat to Chester. Well, if you change your mind…"

"I'll let you know. Thanks."

She resumed her walk. A dog. Maddy would be thrilled. But Chester… Her phone vibrated in her pocket. Her mother. She should have left the phone at home.

"Hi, Mom."

"Did you talk to your friend?"

"I was going to tell you all about it at dinner tonight. The Watuga police think they found the cabin where..."

"They found it! Did they find Amy?"

"No, Mom. The cabin had been burnt to the ground. Nothing's left to identify who was living there."

"Were there bodies?"

"No. In fact, the police think the fire was set deliberately, like the kidnapper was trying to hide any evidence he was there."

"Who owned the cabin?"

She hadn't thought of that angle. "I don't know."

"The police have to find out. Maybe it's a family cabin or there's a deed somewhere."

"I'm sure they're looking into everything. The victim's family, I'm sure, wants them to find this guy as much as we do."

"Do you have an address?"

"No. And stay put. We'll meet you at the inn for dinner tonight. There are some cute shops downtown. Why don't you and Drew have a little fun while you're here."

"Getting Drew to shop is like getting the wind to sit still."

"Then go by yourself. I'd join you, but I really need to get some work done. See you tonight? Around six?"

"See you tonight."

Chapter 6

"Maddy, come on. We're meeting my mother and Drew for dinner."

Maddy came out of her room sporting leggings and an oversized t-shirt. "I want to stay here. I can make my own dinner."

"But you love Coralee's food. Besides, it's a chance to get to know your gran... I mean, my mother."

Henry came in from the kitchen. "We ready to go? Maddy, you're not wearing that, are you?"

"She doesn't want to come," said Emily.

Henry said, "Maddy, get dressed. You can't stay here alone."

"I stay alone all the time."

Emily said, "She's right, but I'd still like her to come with us."

Henry said, "Your grandmother's only here for a short time. It won't kill you to share a meal."

"She's not my grandmother. You just don't want me to..." Maddy stopped, mid-sentence. "It's not like I'm going to get into trouble." She glared at Henry.

Emily said, "We have to go or we'll be late. Mom's a stickler for punctuality. If Maddy doesn't want to come and prefers eating left-overs to Coralee's cooking, so be it."

Henry said, "Okay." While Emily grabbed her sweater, he whispered to Maddy. "No prison phone calls. Letters either."

Maddy huffed off toward her room.

Henry held the Jeep door open for Emily. "How was your visit with Lisa Cutler? Did her daughter get here yet?"

"Shari got here last night. She's very pregnant and didn't get much sleep. I hope all this stress won't affect the baby."

"How's Lisa doing?"

"About like you'd expect. Oh, Shari remembers the hospital where the implant surgery took place but not the doctor's name."

"If we know the hospital, shouldn't be too difficult to find."

"Can't you trace the device by the serial number?"

"It was too mangled to tell. Pat gave it to the police. The crime lab might have better luck."

"I have the name of the person Toby was suing. That's a starting place." She remembered she was supposed to drop that off at the police station. She'd put it on her to-do list for tomorrow.

"You have been busy. Get much writing done?"

She sighed. "You know better than to ask. Do you know what's going on with Maddy? I don't ever remember her giving up a chance to eat at Coralee's and to visit the cats in the café."

"She's a teenager. Whatever it is she'll get over it." He pulled into the parking lot. "I'm hungry. Let's go."

Frances and Drew were waiting in the lobby when they arrived. Coralee promptly seated them near the window overlooking the golf course. "Where's Maddy? We got a litter of kittens today. Thought she'd love to play with them."

Henry said, "Next time. She was in a mood."

Frances sipped her water. "Emily was the moodiest teenager ever. Especially when it got to be around that time of the month. Once a boy at school told her she looked like, what was it again? A pregnant elephant. She didn't leave her room for an entire weekend."

Emily felt like punching her. Maybe it was better Maddy had stayed home. When the waitress took their drink orders, Emily asked for a beer and a shot of Tequila.

Drew said, "How's the meatloaf? Should I order that or the chicken?"

"I recommend the meatloaf," said Henry. He looked at Emily. "Delicious if you eat meat." *If Maddy were here, she'd make a comment about cannibalism.*

Frances said, "Did you talk to Susan? Can her daughter find out who owns the cabin that burnt down?"

"Mom, Lynette is busy with her own detective job. Maybe we can search public records or something."

Henry said, "Did you and Drew get a chance to explore Sugarbury Falls? There are some beautiful covered bridges. It's getting to be picnic weather. Coralee can pack you a lunch to-go."

Picnic weather? Got to bless Henry for trying. Emily sipped her beer.

"We went downtown and browsed in the bookstore."

"And the candy shop," added Drew.

"If you like candy, you should ride out to the outlet mall. The Sugar-buried shop is nationally recognized. Best almond bark ever," said Emily.

Coralee brought the food over personally. "Meatloaf, meatloaf, chicken potpie, and pasta primavera. I'll send the waitress over to refill those drinks."

Emily said, "Coralee, do you know a man named Charlie Adams?"

"I don't recognize the name. Why?"

"Toby Cutler was suing him for neglecting his duty to keep the post office steps clear."

"Oh, that's who you're talking about. Didn't know the fella's name.

There was a bunch of whispering going on when word got out the post-office was being sued. I made sure my front steps were cleared every morning after that. I mean, not that I didn't before."

"When an accident happens, we all turn vigilant—at least for a while," said Emily.

"And the blame game starts. Someone gets hurt, it has to be someone's fault. And they have to be punished. That's the mentality these days, just watch the news," said Coralee.

"Why were they whispering?" asked Emily.

"Folks felt sorry for Charlie. I heard the man was barely surviving on his meager salary as a part-time custodian. Folks say he was out there every morning sweeping leaves or shoveling snow. It didn't make sense he'd leave the steps covered in ice."

"According to the paperwork, Toby was suing the post office as well." Emily twirled her pasta around her fork.

Henry said, "Now there's some deep pockets. It's a federal agency."

Drew said, "Something similar happened where I worked. Computer parts were lying around and a co-worker of mine slipped on them. He was in bad shape, but wound up settling with the company. Never had to work again."

"Looks like neither Charlie nor the post office has anything to worry about now that Toby's dead," said Emily. "I wonder if Charlie has an alibi."

"Benefitting from someone's death isn't the same as killing them," said Frances.

"Emily, how long will Lisa's daughter be in town?" asked Henry.

"She didn't say."

"Did her husband come with her?"

"No, I didn't see him. Why?"

"I don't know. I'm thinking the family may be able to sue even though Toby is dead. I'm sure money's going to be tight, especially with funeral expenses and a baby on the way."

"Good point. After things settle down, I'll tell her to look into it."

Coralee came by. "Anyone for dessert?" Emily was a tad disappointed when everyone chimed in with how full they were. Personally, she was almost never too full for a little dessert.

Coralee said to Frances, "Do you still want directions to the cinema?"

Frances looked at her watch. "Yes. We have time to make the show."

"What show?"

Frances said, "When we were downtown earlier, I noticed a charming cinema. They're showing a special presentation of *Apollo 13*. Drew's a space buff. Do you and Henry want to come along?"

"No, I think we need to get home to Maddy," said Henry.

It was unusual for Henry to give a second thought to leaving Maddy at home. *Perhaps he's had enough of chit-chatting with my mother and a virtual stranger. I have.*

She encouraged the break. "The theater looks like something out of the fifties, you'll see. They even have a live organist who plays before the show starts."

"And the popcorn is still a dollar," said Henry, jumping on the bandwagon. "Even if you don't like the movie you can enjoy a cheap snack." Henry stood up and grabbed the check. Drew took it out of his hand.

"I've got this."

"No, our treat."

"I insist," said Drew. He took out a wad of hundreds.

"Do you need a ride?" said Emily.

"We'll take our car. I'll talk to you tomorrow unless you hear anything else from your friend, Susan."

"I'll call you if I do," said Emily.

Back in the Jeep, Henry said, "Why don't you text Maddy and make sure she's okay."

"I'm sure she's fine, but okay." Within minutes, Maddy had answered that she was working on a school project. "You know what we haven't done in ages?"

"I can think of one thing I'd like to do more often if that's a suggestion."

"We haven't gone out for a drink."

"You just had a drink. Make that two. When have we ever gone out for a drink?"

"My point exactly."

"Tell me what's on your mind."

"Kurt says Charlie Adams is a regular over at Ralph's. My curiosity is getting the best of me. I want to see this guy."

"And what? Ask if he killed Toby?"

"Not in so many words. Just one drink."

"One drink." Henry turned the Jeep around and headed toward town.

A sign barely visible from the road read *Ralp 's*. Was it that difficult to replace the missing H? Emily couldn't understand how a business, even a local bar, would allow itself to make such a sloppy impression.

Henry pulled into the lot in front. A string of twinkling white lights framed the door of the weathered bar, located just shy of downtown. A blue-collar crowd sat on stools, drinking beer and watching a baseball game on the small TV behind the bar. Emily's shoes stuck to the floor and crunched as she maneuvered over the blanket of peanut shells. The juke box blared country western music which made her ears feel like they were under siege by a swarm of twangy mosquitos. She headed toward the row of booths.

"Sure you don't want to sit at the bar?" asked Henry.

"No, I'm good." She leaned her arm on the sticky table.

"How will you know Charlie anyway?"

She didn't have an answer. Not until Kurt walked in.

"Emily and Henry? I've never seen you two in here before. I didn't think this was your kind of watering hole."

"You wouldn't be wrong," said Emily. "I'd rather be sipping a latte at a coffeehouse, but I was hoping to get a glimpse of Charlie Adams. Is he here?"

"Don't see him yet. He usually shows up later." He squeezed into the booth next to Henry. "Did you have dinner with your parents, Emily?"

"With my mother and her husband. They went to catch a movie downtown."

"You give any more thought to the puppies?"

Henry said, "What puppies?"

"I saw Kurt while I was running this morning and mentioned it'd be nice to have a four-legged companion."

"You have Chester."

"Not exactly a running buddy. Kurt's neighbor's dog is expecting a litter."

Kurt looked at the door. "That's him. That's Charlie. He's going straight for the pool table."

Henry took a swig of his beer. When Emily banged his knee under the table, he caught her drift. "Uh, want to play?"

"You play pool?" said Kurt.

"Not very well."

"Spoken like one of them pool sharks. Come on."

Emily followed them to the table where Charlie had just racked up the balls.

Charlie said, "Kurt, want in?"

"Yeah. My neighbor Henry, too. He's here with his wife, Emily."

"Are we playing for money?"

Henry said, "Not me. I'm a bit rusty."

They began the game. Emily looked Charlie over. Medium height, medium build, wearing a gray hoodie! He was wearing work boots. The footprint she saw on the roof looked more like sneaker prints, but she wasn't an expert. Besides, people own more than one pair of shoes. Good Lord, she had at least a dozen in her closet.

Henry said, "We can't stay long. I've got some work to do regarding Toby Cutler." Emily smiled at him. She was trying to figure out a way to bring Toby's name into the conversation.

"It's too bad about his tragic death," said Emily. *Did that sound too random*?

"Sure is," said Charlie. "Research?"

"I'm a doctor." He came up with a quick fib. "The hospital had me fill out a report. I was first on the scene."

Did she imagine it, or did Charlie tear up just a little at the sound of Toby's name? She played dumb. "The two of you were friends?"

"Hated the guy. He tried to ruin my life. My wife and I are barely scraping by. One more late payment and I lose my car. Suing me for negligence? I shoveled those steps that morning."

"So in a way, it's a relief that he's dead," said Emily.

"I never said that. Wouldn't wish murder on my worst enemy."

"How do you know it was murder?"

Charlie took his shot, then said, "I don't. I'm just going by what I heard on the news. They said it was a suspicious death. I watch them cop shows. Suspicious death means murder."

"We were there when it happened, like Henry said. Couldn't believe it. One minute we're looking at pottery, the next, someone's screaming and there's a man splattered on the ground. Were you at the arts fair?"

"No. Not my idea of a fun weekend. I was home watching the game."

"Alone?"

"Your turn," said Kurt.

While Charlie lined up his shot, Henry shook his head at Emily and mimed 'don't grill him like that.'

Charlie took his turn.

"Nice shot," said Henry.

"Good thing you didn't bet money," said Kurt. "He's the real pool shark."

"Are you married, Charlie?" asked Emily.

"Yep. Going on twenty years."

"Did your wife go to the arts fair?"

"My wife was visiting her sister last weekend. What's with all the questions?"

Henry said, "She was a reporter in another life. She can't help herself. I've gotta go to work tomorrow. Come on, Emily."

"Okay. Nice meeting you, Charlie."

Henry started the Jeep. "What's your impression?"

"You were right. You're a terrible pool player."

"Ha-ha. About Charlie."

"Seems like a normal guy but that doesn't mean anything. Ted Bundy's neighbors thought he was a great guy and he turned out to be a serial killer." Emily scrolled through her phone messages.

"He didn't seem nervous or anything when you asked where he was during the fair."

"And he almost looked upset at first. He doesn't have an alibi and he has a strong motive."

"Nothing places him at the crime scene."

"He was wearing a gray hoodie tonight."

"Seriously? I'll bet half the people you talk to own a gray hoodie." He pulled into their driveway. "Lights are on. Looks like Maddy's still up."

He unlocked the front door. At that moment, Maddy clicked off the TV.

"What are you watching?" asked Henry.

"Nothing. I'm going to bed."

Emily said, "Did you find something for dinner?"

"I called for pizza. There's leftover in the fridge if you're hungry."

"I'm still full from dinner," said Emily. "Goodnight."

"Goodnight," said Maddy.

"Goodnight, Maddy," said Henry. She ignored him, scooped up Chester, and went to her room.

Henry grabbed the remote.

"Are you going to stay up and watch TV?" asked Emily.

"I want to see what she was watching. She acted like she was hiding something."

"Since when are you so suspicious? I'm going to bed."

"Okay." He looked at the screen. Just as he thought. *Prison Bound.* She had been watching a documentary, no, make that a reality show, about prisoners.

Chapter 7

The next morning, Henry left early for work. Toby's daughter had jotted down the name of the hospital and given it to Emily yesterday. He hoped to find the doctor who inserted the ICD. He took the paper out of his pocket. Hmm. He had met one of the cardiac surgeons from a hospital in Coral Way a few years back at a medical conference and they'd been playing *Words with Friends* online ever since.

"Morgan? It's Henry Fox, from Vermont."

"Hen128? The radiologist from New York? You know I had nothing but vowels that entire last game or I'd have beaten you."

"Luck of the draw. We're in Vermont now, but yes, it's me. I was hoping you could help."

"If I knew a good 2-letter word starting with the letter C, I wouldn't tell you."

"There aren't any. That's not why I'm calling. We had a guy plunge off a roof on Saturday. We can't figure out if he jumped, was pushed, or had a heart attack and lost his balance. Anyhow, during the autopsy, we found an ICD. The daughter says it was implanted at your hospital and doesn't remember the name of the doctor."

"Let me get my laptop open. Okay. What's his name?"

"Toby Cutler."

"The name doesn't ring a bell. Let me do a search."

"It was last year some time."

"Hmm. Nope. He's not in the database."

"Are you sure? T-o-b-y C-u"

"I can spell. No, he isn't in here."

"Is there a nearby hospital that does this surgery?"

"This hospital is the first choice for that procedure. The nearest hospital is a small community hospital."

"Okay. Thanks. Everything going well for you?"

"Yeah. I'm heading to the conference in St. Louis at the end of the month. Are you going to be there?"

"No. I'm semi-retired. Haven't been to a conference since we moved to Vermont. And don't take it too hard when you see the word I put on the triple word score. Used all 7 letters and it has a Z on a triple letter as well."

"You're bluffing."

"Am I? Take care. Thanks for your time."

Toby's daughter told Emily she was sure of the name of the hospital when she jotted it down. Why wasn't he in the hospital database? He called the nearby community hospital. Toby had never been a patient there either.

"Knock, knock." Pat came in balancing two cups of coffee.

"Hey, buddy. What do you need?"

"What do I need? I came by to say hello before heading to the morgue."

"If you come bearing coffee, you're always welcome. Did you guys find a venue the other day?"

"We saw a beautiful place. They have an outdoor area with a waterfall in the background. Megan thinks it's a great backdrop for pictures."

"Did you put down a deposit?"

"They're booked through next year."

"Seriously?"

"Yeah. But as we were discussing it with the manager, he gets a call and has a cancellation. What are the chances?"

"So you took it, right? When's the date?"

Pat cleared his throat. "A week from Saturday."

"You're kidding, right? How are you going to get a wedding together so quickly?"

"Megan's already got a dress. She ordered bridesmaid dresses, too, for Emily and Maddy as well as her friend Kim at the station. She called the shop and they're going to put a rush on the order."

"What about the flowers and a DJ, and a cake?"

"The venue handles all that. We're doing a cake tasting tomorrow evening."

"Congrats! You going to have those coated almonds tied in the net bags? Love the pink ones, myself."

"If you're volunteering to make them."

"Guess I've got to get measured for my tux."

"Yep. Me too. We'll find a time to go over in the next few days."

"It's a plan. Emily and Maddy will be so excited. Hey. What if it rains?"

"They have an indoor area just in case. See ya, buddy."

He sipped his coffee and googled ICD recalls. Maybe the machine malfunctioned. Nothing. He glanced at his watch. Time to get to the emergency department.

***

Emily stopped at the police station first thing in the morning. She felt guilty keeping the lawsuit information to herself overnight. She peeked behind the counter and motioned to Megan.

"Emily, come on in."

"You're not busy?"

"I've got a little time."

"Toby's wife gave me this folder full of information on the lawsuit. The guy Toby was suing is named Charlie Adams. He's suing the city as well."

Megan skimmed through the folder. "I'm on it. I'll pay Charlie Adams a visit this afternoon."

"We met him at Ralph's last night."

"Ralph's? Since when do you hang out at bars?"

"Kurt mentioned Charlie was kind of a regular so after dinner we stopped by. He's medium height and build. He was wearing work boots and a gray hoodie."

"That meshes with what the witness described, but that description could fit a lot of people."

"It was strange…"

"What was strange?" asked Megan.

"I don't know. You'd think Charlie would have been elated that Toby is dead. He seemed almost sad. Either he'd had enough to drink that he was chill, as Maddy would say, or he's naturally easy going. Anyhow, you'll see for yourself."

Megan smiled. "I have news. We found a wedding venue."

"You did? Where?"

"The Tory House, by the waterfall. They have a gorgeous garden with a gazebo. I hadn't thought about saying our vows outside until I saw it."

"It's a popular venue. I'll bet they're booked for the rest of the year."

"Longer. But fate stepped in. While we were talking to the manager, they got a cancellation."

"Fantastic. When's the date?"

"A week from Saturday."

"Did you just say a week from Saturday? I'm sure that's not what I heard."

"It's then or wait two years. We've got the dresses already. We hadn't sent out invitations yet."

"Our dresses won't be ready. They have to be fitted and then altered."

"I put a rush on them. I'm so excited. The venue will handle the food and flowers. I'm going to be married in ten days."

Emily hugged her. "Congratulations. It was meant to be. Let me know if you need help with anything."

The post office was only a few doors down from the police station. Emily took a short detour on the way to her car and stopped in front of the older building with the steep, stone steps. She could believe someone would be hurt pretty badly if they slipped off of them like Toby did. She heard Charlie got fired after the incident. She wondered if she'd get more information if she went inside.

She got in line behind an elderly lady trying to mail a package. When finished, she said to the man in the window, "Hi, I'm a reporter and I'm doing a story on the lawsuit involving Charlie Adams. Is it true he forgot to clear the steps the day the Toby Cutler fell?" *Once a reporter, always a reporter, even if I am retired from the newspaper.*

"Ma'am, we were told specifically not to talk about the case."

"But now that Toby Cutler is dead, the case has been dropped. Charlie and the city are both off the hook."

"Then there's no story."

"Correct." She read his badge. Although she wrote non-fiction, she had an incredibly creative side to her. "You're correct, Tim. The story I'm doing is on the obligations businesses have toward keeping their customers safe. I've met Charlie. Sweet man. I'm sure he didn't purposely neglect his duties and I'd like to put that in my article."

"Charlie's as good as they get. Never missed a day of work and took his job seriously. Every morning first thing when he came in he swept the steps or shoveled them if it had snowed. I think this Toby fellow was faking the whole thing."

"So the steps weren't icy when this happened?"

"We'd had freezing rain the night before. I can't say if the steps were slippery because I go in the back entrance. I'm pretty sure I saw Charlie go out there."

"Pretty sure, or positive?"

"Like I said, he cleared the steps every morning."

"Is there anyone here I can talk to who witnessed the accident?"

"Marco the mail carrier is coming through the door now. He was the one who called the ambulance."

By this time, a line had formed behind her. The elderly lady behind her cleared her throat quite deliberately.

"Thank you for your help, Tim."

"Let us know when the article comes out."

Emily caught Marco the mail carrier just before he went to the back.

"Excuse me. My name is Emily Fox and I'm writing an article on workplace safety." She pulled one of her business cards from her purse, hoping he wouldn't notice it said college professor/author. He skimmed over the card.

"We aren't allowed to talk about it. I've got work to do."

Emily wasn't about to give up. "Tim says you saw the accident they were trying to pin on poor Charlie Adams. You called the ambulance, correct? Good thing. If you hadn't acted so quickly, who knows how much worse he'd have been."

"Yeah, I called, but I didn't actually see the guy fall down the steps."

"The steps were icy, right?"

"Yeah. I come in through the front every day. I almost slipped myself."

"And the steps are generally clear?"

"Always. Charlie was right on it and he got here right at the start of our work day, always before me. That was the first time I ever found them slippery like that."

"And the man who fell, was he unconscious?"

"No. He was just lying there saying how his back hurt and he couldn't move his neck. The EMTs came and put one of them collars around his neck and put him on one of those boards like on TV."

"Did anyone take pictures of the accident scene?"

"I saw a few phones going. I don't know after that. One thing's been bothering me."

"What's that?"

"The steps were so slippery, but the side walk right in front wasn't. Charlie was responsible for that, too."

"Really? Like he was working on clearing the area in front of the post office and got interrupted? Maybe he forgot he hadn't finished."

"I don't know. Maybe. Aren't you supposed to take notes or something?"

She pointed to her head. "I've got it all up here. I'll drop the article by when it comes out."

She headed back to the car. *When it comes out?* She hoped those two would forget because there certainly wasn't going to be an article. Since she'd left her job as a crime reporter back in New York and turned her attention to writing true crime novels, she hadn't written so much as a freelance article.

Why was the sidewalk clear but not the steps? Had Marco remembered correctly? She had no real schedule today. She fished in her purse for the copies she made before turning the legal folder over to the police. Aha. She found the name of Charlie's defense attorney and plugged the address into her GPS.

Chapter 8

When she arrived at the free-standing legal office, she checked the name on the shingle against what was on the paperwork. Frank Marango. This was the right place. She walked in expecting a secretary gatekeeper, but instead found a middle-aged man typing at a desktop computer facing the back wall.

"Excuse me. I'm looking for Frank Marango."

He nearly jumped out of his chair. "You startled me. I'm Frank Marango. What can I do for you?"

"I'm Emily Fox, reporter. I'm working on an article about lawsuits related to negligence. You were Charlie Adams's defense lawyer, correct?"

"Charlie, yeah. I was. Poor guy. Guess he's off the hook now."

"Do you think he was guilty of neglect?"

"Who are you again? What paper do you work for?"

"I'm writing a freelance article. I'll sell to the highest bidder."

"You get any ID like a badge or something?"

"I can mention your firm. All publicity is good publicity, right?" He seemed satisfied with her answer.

"Why don't you talk to Charlie?"

"I plan to. I want to get all the angles."

"I'd never throw a client, even an ex-client, under the bus, but... Charlie didn't remember a single witness who could verify he salted the steps to remove the ice, like he said he did."

"In fact, I was at the post office and it seems there were witnesses to say the steps were slippery," said Emily.

"I know all about it. Charlie pointed me right to those witnesses."

"Do you have pictures of the accident scene?"

He fished through the files on his desk. "Yeah. Here."

Emily looked at the photos carefully, zeroing in on the sidewalk in front of the steps. With difficulty, she was able to make out ice on the post office steps. She couldn't be sure about the sidewalk.

"Honestly, I tried to get him to settle. I'm good at my job, but we really didn't have much of a defense. Witnesses saw the guy fall and we had medical reports documenting the injuries sustained by Toby Cutler."

Emily looked at the medical reports which were signed by a local chiropractor. "Charlie didn't want to settle and put this behind him? He stood to lose a lot of money."

"That's what I'm saying. He wanted to have his day in court. Wanted to prove he wasn't negligent."

"Okay. Guess that wasn't in the cards. Can I take one of those photos? The one of the steps and sidewalk."

He hesitated for a moment. "I'm not sure I should…"

"I could use it for the article."

"I suppose it doesn't matter now. Okay. Help yourself."

"Can I make a copy of the medical report?"

"No can do. Privacy laws and all that."

"I understand. Thanks for your help. It's M-A-R-A-N-G-O, right?" She spelled out the name.

"That's it."

Once in the car, she phoned Henry. "You busy?"

"I've got a few minutes between patients. What's up?"

"I just got done doing a little investigating. Charlie Adams's lawyer said Charlie wasn't anxious to settle because he wanted his day in court to prove his innocence. Maybe Charlie doubted the severity of Toby's injuries. The lawyer had an injury report from a local chiropractor. Can you check the emergency room records for comparison?"

"There are doctors and chiropractors out there who'll exaggerate the injuries for a price. Let me check." He took more than a few minutes to get the information. "Okay, Toby Cutler was treated and released the day of the accident. He had x-rays and some other tests, but nothing severe enough to get him admitted."

"Not even a broken wrist or a twisted ankle?"

"No, but some injuries show up later. Whiplash, chronic back pain, headaches..."

"The report the lawyer had showed serious injuries. Do you know a chiropractor named Tom Willis?"

"Can't say I do. I'll ask around if you want."

"Yes, please do."

"Okay. Did you hear Pat and Megan are getting married in ten days?"

"Yes, Megan told me when I dropped off the information on the law suit. Good for them."

"Yeah. Pat's waited long enough to be happy again. I might go by the formalwear store with him after work, seeing as I'm the best man. Should I be doing anything else? He doesn't want a bachelor party."

"Just be supportive. Make sure he's got the rings on the big day, and that he's filed for a marriage license. Oh, and you'll have to make a toast so start working on it. Let me know if you find out anything about the chiropractor. Love you."

"Love you, too."

Emily wanted to make one more stop before heading home. She called her neighbors, Rebecca and Abby.

"Hi, Rebecca. Is Abby home? I was wondering if she could enlarge a photo for me."

"She's doing a shoot but she'll be home in an hour or so."

"I'll stop by then if it's okay."

"You're always welcome here."

Emily went home and made herself a late lunch which she ate with Chester on her lap.

"Chester, you know how much I love you and you'll always be my baby, but...how would you feel about having a dog around?"

Chester bumped against her hand. She took it as a sign he was okay with the idea. Maddy would be ecstatic. Henry on the other hand...

After lunch, she sat down to work on her book. When she stopped to look at the time, several hours had passed. Maddy would be home from school soon. She grabbed the photo she'd gotten from the lawyer and walked over to Abby and Rebecca's cabin.

Abby and Rebecca's cabin was one of the homiest and most tastefully done homes Emily had ever been in. When Abby opened the door, the aroma of vanilla from the candle on the coffee table brought back memories of baking cookies with her mother...before Amy drowned, or should she say, disappeared?

"Hi, Emily. Come on in. Rebecca's doing some work upstairs."

"She's so willing to help whenever I drop by, I almost forget she has her own full time job to keep up with. Whatever that is." Emily thought CIA, maybe a spy...

"I don't know all the details, either. Cyber security, background checks...I don't ask any more."

"Well, this time I was hoping *you* could help." She pulled the photo out of the manila envelope. "Is there any way to enlarge this or make it clearer? I'm trying to determine whether there was ice on the sidewalk or just on the steps."

Abby took the picture. "I can certainly enlarge it. Can't guarantee the clarity."

"That'd be great, thanks."

Milo, their black and white Border Collie, trotted down the stairs.

"I guess he was helping Rebecca," said Emily. "I was thinking about getting a dog. Kurt's neighbor has a dog that's expecting puppies and trying to find them homes."

"You mean Edgar? I hope you have deep pockets."

"What do you mean"

"Those puppies will be pedigreed. That translates to expensive. Anyway, why do you want some designer puppy when the shelters are full of dogs needing homes?"

"I didn't realize those puppies were specially bred. I thought the dog got pregnant and Edgar was stuck finding them homes."

"No, don't worry. He'll sell those puppies in a heartbeat and make a nice profit."

"Maybe I'll take Maddy and check out the shelter."

"There's an animal rescue just outside of town as well. You'll be giving a dog a chance at a life."

"Thanks, Abby. If I can talk Henry into it, I'll go check it out."

"Give me a little time and I'll get the picture to you."

"Will do. Tell Rebecca I said hello."

The walk home helped her solidify the next chapter of her work in progress. Spring break, more like late winter break, would be ending soon, and although her part time teaching position at St. Edwards didn't exactly eat up all her time, it was nice not to be planning and grading writing examples. If she were to get a dog, would it be better to get one before her vacation ended, or to wait until summer? First things first. She and Henry needed to have a discussion before doing anything.

Henry's Jeep wasn't in the driveway, but she hadn't expected him home quite yet. She took off her jacket and was about to make herself a cup of tea, when her mother called.

"Emily, I have an idea to help find Amy."

"Mom? What idea?"

"I was watching one of those morning talk shows and they were talking about hypnotism. They even talked to a woman who was able to identify the man who robbed her after remembering details under hypnosis."

"Mom, that's crazy. It was thirty years ago and I didn't see anything."

"Can't you try? They said memories get buried deeply but they're all tucked away in the subconscious."

"I don't even believe in hypnosis."

"It's not about making people bark like dogs when they hear a code word. Ask your detective friend. Police use it to solve crimes."

"They also use psychics when they're desperate," said Emily.

"It's not the same. I'll pay for the hypnosis. I'll ask Coralee here at the inn if she knows anyone, or better yet, ask your detective friend who they use."

If she was going to ask anyone, it'd be Henry, but that was beside the point. "I doubt the police department has a hypnotist on speed dial. Besides, I don't want to be hypnotized. I thought I'd made that clear. Let's hope the Watuga police find them and even more important, let's hope it's really Amy. I don't want to get my hopes up and be crushed all over again when they find them and it isn't her. Maddy will be home soon. You and Drew are coming for dinner later, right?"

"Yes. Just think about it, okay?"

"I'll think about it, but it won't change how I feel. I'll see you at dinner."

Emily checked the fridge to be sure the zucchini and mushrooms she'd bought a few days ago were still fresh. She had ricotta cheese, mozzarella, lasagna noodles, eggs…She opened the pantry and pulled out a Mason jar of tomato sauce she'd canned last summer.

"Emily? I'm home." Maddy tossed her backpack on the counter. "What are you making?"

"Vegetable lasagna. My mother and Drew are coming for dinner. How was school?" She put a pot of water on the stove.

"Fine. Oh, I checked social media for you. I think we can figure out who the witness is. You know, the one who was kidnapped."

"How?"

"I found an old post from a girl in Watuga. She was asking for help finding her missing sister. She posted a picture of the sister and asked people to share. You know, one of those pictures that goes viral?"

"How do you know it's her?"

"I've never been to Watuga but even when I lived in Chicago I can't remember hearing about any kidnappings. I guess it could be a coincidence. Never mind."

"No! Show me."

Maddy took her phone out of her backpack. "Look, here's the post. About a week later, there's another post saying how happy she was that her sister was found alive."

Emily looked over the posts and picture. "I'll bet you're right. It can't be a coincidence. How many kidnappings does one town get?"

"Well, don't judge crime rate based on Sugarbury Falls." Maddy opened the pantry and grabbed a granola bar, then foraged in the fridge. "Are we out of almond milk?"

"No, look in the back." Emily enlarged the image on the phone with her fingers. "The name of the missing girl is Kathleen O'Malley. Can you respond to the post?"

"And say what?"

Emily jumped when Henry walked in. He put his lunch box on the counter and gave her a kiss. "What are you looking at, Em? Better not be naked pictures of George Clooney again. You know he's married now."

"Very funny." Emily showed him the picture. "Look what Maddy found. I think we've figured out the identity of the mysterious kidnapping victim. If we can contact her…"

"How crazy. I thought they hid her identity because they feared for her safety."

Maddy said, "When they posted this she wasn't a kidnapping victim. She was just a missing person and they were desperate to find her."

Emily said, "Can you write back and see if her sister would be willing to talk to us?"

"Maybe you should. You're the writer. I don't know what to say without sounding like a stalker."

"Okay. I have to start dinner, then I'll draft it." She hugged Maddy. "You're amazing; you know that?"

"Yeah, yeah. I'm going to start my homework before company gets here." She grabbed her backpack and went to her room.

Henry said, "She seems in an okay mood."

"Yeah. She really helped us by searching social media."

"If you get a response and if you can talk to the victim, and if she tells you something you don't already know…"

"I get it. We don't know how credible she is. Now, go change your clothes and you can peel the zucchini." She preheated the oven and threw the noodles in the water. Then she fiddled with writing a post, trying to sound authentic but not like a psycho chasing rainbows. She stopped to assemble and bake the lasagna.

"Want me to toss the salad?" said Henry.

"Sure. Does this sound okay?"

He read what she'd written on the back of a used envelope. "That'll work. I'll get this salad and the bread out on the table. They'll be here shortly."

"I think I hear a car outside. I'll get the door."

Frances and Drew arrived with a box of chocolates.

"We took your advice and rode over to the outlet mall. These are from the Sugar-buried shop. You were right. Best chocolate I've ever tasted," said Frances.

Drew said, "She's right." He exaggerated a breath. "Something smells good."

"I made a vegetable lasagna and salad. Nothing fancy. Come in and have a seat." She knocked on Maddy's door. "Maddy, our guests are here."

Maddy sat down on the sofa next to Frances. "Emily, did you tell her about the post?"

"What post?" said Frances.

"I went on social media and found a picture of the girl who was kidnapped. Emily's going to respond to the post and see if she can talk to the girl who saw Amy."

Frances said, "Oh my God. We're getting closer, I feel it."

"First of all, it's the girl who *thinks* she saw Amy. And that's if she even responds. Don't get your hopes up, Mom." She wished she'd warned Maddy not to say anything yet.

"Have you thought any more about the hypnosis?"

"What hypnosis?" said Henry.

"Mom saw a show about how hypnosis helps in remembering things our minds have buried. She thinks if I get hypnotized, I'll remember something about Amy's disappearance."

Maddy said, "We learned about hypnosis in my biology class."

"That's what they're spending time teaching you? The course isn't rigorous enough?" said Emily.

"No, really it works. It doesn't hurt or do damage to your brain or anything. You should do it."

Emily stood up. "Dinner's ready. Come on before it gets cold."

"Emily, are we out of napkins?" asked Henry.

"No, I'll get some from the pantry. Be right back." She dug through the shelves, noticing the package of napkins had fallen under the bottom shelf. *Good thing the floor is clean.* She knelt on the floor and stretched her arm under as far as she could.

As they were getting settled at the table, Drew's phone buzzed. "Excuse me. I have to take this. I'll be quick." He took the phone into the kitchen, not noticing Emily crouched on the floor behind the counter, digging through the bottom of the pantry.

Drew said, "Look, you're a fool for not accepting. If you don't change your mind soon things could heat up big time. Watch your back." He stuck the phone in his pocket and went to the table. *What was that all about?* Emily followed, carrying the napkins.

Frances said, "Henry just told us about the detective's wedding. Ten days! That's quick."

Drew said, "Quick? We decided to get married in the morning and had flown to Vegas and tied the knot before sundown."

"Not the same thing. The drive-thru chapel we went to didn't require a whole lot of preparation," said Frances.

Maddy said, "How long did you know each other before you got engaged?"

Frances looked at Drew, Drew looked at Frances. They both laughed and answered, "Three days."

Frances said, "It was love at first sight. Sometimes you just know." She squeezed Drew's hand.

Henry cleared his throat and looked at Maddy. "Maybe that's true when you're older and experienced. It's important to evaluate the decision as to choosing a life partner very carefully, Maddy. It takes time to get to know what someone is really like."

Maddy rolled her eyes at him.

Drew said, "The lasagna is fabulous. Don't even miss the meat."

Frances said, "Emily, I never expected you to stop eating meat. Remember how you used to scarf down those fast food burgers on ten-cent Tuesdays?" She looked at Maddy. "Your mother made herself so sick one time she threw up all over the restaurant."

"It was a fast food joint, not a restaurant," said Emily.

"Well, you certainly are slimmer these days. Is it from being a vegetarian?"

It was Emily's turn to roll her eyes. Her phone buzzed. "I'll be right back." Normally she would have let it go to voicemail, but she was happy to leave an embarrassing moment behind. Certainly slimmer? She wasn't exactly a porker growing up, though to her mother, anything short of a model's physique was overweight.

"Abby? What's up? Were you able to enlarge the photo?"

"Yes, and you were right. There is definitely ice on the steps, but not on the sidewalk."

"You're sure?"

"Yes. You can come and pick it up. See for yourself."

"My mother and her husband are here for dinner. I'll come by in the morning. Thanks a million."

"Any time. Now, get back to your dinner."

Emily went back to the table. Maddy was telling Drew and Frances all about the cat café she'd started as a school project.

Drew said, "I'm more of a dog man."

"Do you have a dog?" asked Maddy.

"No, but I had a boxer growing up. He was like my shadow. Our place is too small for a dog. They need room to run around. Maybe once we move."

Emily said, "I was thinking of getting a dog."

Maddy's face brightened; Henry's fell.

"Really?" said Henry. "That's the first I've heard you mention a dog."

Maddy said, "I'd love to have a dog. Let's go to the shelter tomorrow and look."

Henry said, "What brought this on?"

"Kurt's neighbor's dog is expecting a litter. Kurt thought he needed to find homes. Come to find out from Abby, those are expensive dogs, specially bred. Abby said I should give a rescue or shelter dog a home and I think she's right."

"Remember when our neighbor's dog chased you on your bike and you got so scared you crashed into a telephone pole? How many stiches did you wind up with again? Oh, and good thing I knew enough to put your tooth in a cup of milk or the dentist wouldn't have been able to put it back in. It was right in the front, too."

"Thanks, Mom. I'm not afraid of dogs anymore. I was thinking a running companion would be fun."

"You know how Chester is about sharing," said Henry. "Besides, a dog really curtails your freedom. You can't just pick up and go away for a weekend."

"I didn't say I'd made a decision, and, of course, all three of us would have to be onboard."

Maddy said, "I'm in. We could always get Kurt or Rebecca, or even Jessica to stop by and take care of the dog for a weekend. I do it for Rebecca and Abby all the time. Milo's no problem."

"Dessert, anyone?" She stood up. "I'll put on the coffee and we've got carrot cake."

"Carrot cake. Guess you're really serious about the vegetarian thing," said Frances.

Emily rushed dessert along, not sure how much more she could tolerate her mother. After they left, she ran over the post she'd drafted and gave it to Maddy.

Maddy said, "I'll put this up now and hopefully we'll get a response. Do you need help cleaning up?"

"Thanks, honey, but Dad and I will get it. Do the post and finish your homework. I'll see you in the morning."

Chapter 9

One more day of Spring break, gone. Emily hoped to have gotten further along in her writing. Once she went back to work, she'd not only have less time to write, but less time to help Megan with the murder investigation, employing her skills as a reporter and true crime writer. Megan and Pat's wedding was fast approaching and she knew Megan wouldn't be able to enjoy it as much with an open murder case sitting on her desk and her partner, Ron Wooster, on vacation.

"Emily, look!" Maddy came into the kitchen with her laptop. "I got an answer. She said to send her a private message and we can arrange a phone call with her sister."

"She answered so quickly? Let me see." She sat at the table with the laptop and absorbed every word. "Tell her to call after school or tonight, or any time after you and Henry are home. Maddy, this might be the break we're waiting for."

Maddy typed a response. "I've got to get to school but I'll check on my phone and text you when she answers."

"Thanks."

After Maddy left, Emily went to visit Lisa Cutler. By now, she was likely in the midst of making funeral arrangements and she didn't know how long her daughter would be in town. When she got to the house, Shari answered the door.

"Mom's still asleep. I hate to wake her."

"No, don't. She needs her rest. I wanted to see if you needed anything. Trying to arrange a funeral can be overwhelming. Are you staying in town long?"

"Not more than another week. I have doctor appointments and things that need to get done before the baby arrives."

"Is your husband coming for the funeral?"

"I'm trying to convince him. He and my dad didn't get along."

"I'm sorry to hear that."

"They got along great when we first started dating, but things changed after the…They changed after a while."

"Do you need help with arrangements? I know your mother's church friend has been helpful."

"We booked the church. Funeral's day after tomorrow. I figured we'd all come back here afterwards, but I have no idea how many people to expect. I don't know if my dad had many friends."

"He hung out at Ralph's bar, according to my neighbor. I'm sure he had a few friends there."

"And he has a high school buddy up here somewhere. It's one of the reasons he chose to relocate here."

"Do you know his buddy's name?"

"No. Mom probably does, though. Wait, I saw an old yearbook on the bookshelf when I was looking for something to read." She went over and pulled it out. "Maybe there's a clue in here." She flipped through the pages. "This is from back in his high school days. Hard to imagine him back then."

"You wouldn't recognize anyone, would you? I know these are from before you were born."

Shari flipped through. "He's got a baseball team picture in here. Looks like everyone signed it on the back."

Emily looked at the photo, then flipped it over and read the names. "Phil, Bert, Charlie, Coach..." Do you recognize any of these people or any of the names?"

"Sorry, no."

Emily looked closely. She might be imagining it, but the boy next to Toby in the photo looked a lot like the Charlie she met at Ralph's. Younger, of course, and with less hair. Suing his best friend?

Lisa came into the room. "I thought I heard voices."

Emily said, "I dropped by to see if you need anything."

"If I do, my head's so jumbled right now I wouldn't even know it."

"Shari was trying to figure out how many people to expect to feed after the funeral. Did Toby have many friends?"

"He'd just started working at the local school as a security guard. We weren't making it on social security and our meager savings. There may be a few people he knows at the school. I'm not sure after him being there such a short time."

Shari said, "You have those church friends. They'll want to be here. How many would you say?"

"I don't know. Maybe a dozen or so. Most of those are my friends but I'm sure they'll want to be there for me."

Emily said, "Shari was telling me about an old high school buddy." She handed her the photo. "Do you know any of these men? Or how to get in touch with the buddy who lives here?"

"No. Don't recognize any of them."

"How about the friend who lives here?"

"What friend? We moved here not knowing a soul."

Shari said, "Mom, remember how Dad heard about Sugarbury Falls? It was from his old high school buddy who lives here."

"I never heard him mention a high school buddy."

"Mom, seriously? You don't remember?"

Emily said, "Did you ever hear him mention a Charlie Adams?"

"Hmm. Charlie Adams is the man Toby was suing. He didn't know him until the accident happened."

"Mom, are you sure you don't recognize anyone? Look at the picture again."

Lisa looked at the page. "I never met Charlie Adams, and, no, that person in the picture doesn't look familiar to me."

"If Toby and Charlie had an issue from the past, and because of the accident, Charlie realized Toby was living here, maybe he had a stronger motive for murder than getting out of being sued." Emily was thinking out loud. There was nothing yet to suggest they'd had a problem from the past.

Lisa said, "Toby didn't know Charlie before the incident happened. Although…"

"Although what? You remember him?"

"Toby was acting a bit strange in the weeks before he died. He got some phone calls which he took in private. Once he got one around midnight and ran right out of the house. He said it was nothing to worry about."

"Mom, why didn't you tell the police?"

"My mind's been so scrambled. I didn't remember."

Emily said, "Could he have been talking to Charlie Adams?"

"I suppose."

"Now we're getting somewhere," said Shari.

"Now that I'm thinking about it, I think Charlie Adams was threatening Toby and trying to make him drop the law suit. We found a note stuck in our door."

"What note, Mom? Do you still have it?"

Lisa rummaged through the desk, throwing scraps of paper onto the floor. "Here it is."

Emily read the note out loud. "You will pay." It was written in red marker with a skull and crossbones under it. "You have to give this to the police. You should have called them as soon as you got this. They might have been able to lift fingerprints."

"I'll make sure they get it," said Shari. "Ouch." She clutched her stomach.

"What's wrong?"

"Nothing's wrong. The baby's kicking up a storm." She smiled.

Emily said, "That's reassuring."

"Do you have children?" asked Shari.

Emily hated that question. "I don't have any *biological* children, but when my college roommate died, I became her daughter's guardian. We now have a fourteen-year-old daughter."

"I hope you live through it. I was a teenage terror. Dad used to…Dad…" Emily saw tears stream down Shari's cheeks. She gave her a hug.

"I'm going to let you go. Call me if you need anything. Shari, you should get some rest."

"I'll try."

When Emily pulled into her driveway, she decided to walk over to Kurt's before going in. She saw his truck in the driveway and knocked on the door.

"Emily, come on in. Edgar's dog had the puppies this morning. Six of them. Little bitty things with their eyes closed. You should go by."

"I haven't sold Henry on the idea of getting a dog, and to be honest, if we do get one, I'm going to make it a rescue dog."

"I got Prancer from a shelter when he was just about a year old." Prancer moved from his position under the kitchen table, to the area rug in front of the sofa. "He knows we're talking about him."

"I didn't know he came from a shelter. He's pure Chocolate Lab, isn't he?"

"He looks like a lab but the vet thought he was a mix. Anyhow, I hit the jackpot."

"You sure did." Prancer licked her hand.

"Can I get you something to eat?"

"No. I want to ask you a few questions about Charlie Adams."

"Charlie from the bar?"

"Yes." She scratched Prancer between the ears. "For one thing, did you get the impression Charlie and Toby knew each other before they met at the bar?"

"I don't know. We all just hang out, play pool, and drink beer. No talking the meaning of life or anything."

"You never saw them talking privately, like they had something they didn't want everyone to hear?"

"Once the whole law suit thing started, neither of them came around much. Charlie starting showing up again after Toby died."

"Think hard. They never mentioned going to school together?"

"School? Nah."

"No whispers or conversations in the rest room?"

"Nope. Wait. Once Toby got real hammered and said he'd 'done something real bad.' Charlie said something strange back to him."

"He did something 'real bad' to Charlie? Maybe he meant suing him."

"Don't think so. Charlie told him it wasn't his fault and gave him a pat on the back."

"Like he was comforting a friend?"

"I guess."

"Has Charlie seemed less stressed since the law suit has gone away?"

"He never seemed stressed when it was going on. He was more stressed after Toby died, in fact. Maybe they were closer than I thought."

"Did Toby say anything about receiving threats?"

"Threats? Not to me he didn't."

She looked at her watch. "Okay, Kurt. Thanks for the info."

"You're back to playing detective again, aren't you?"

"Megan and Pat are getting married a week from Saturday. Detective Wooster is on vacation. I'm trying to take some work off her plate while I'm on Spring Break."

"You're a good friend. Be careful, now. You've had some close ones when you went nosing around those other murders."

"I've learned my lesson. See you later."

Walking back to her cabin, Emily received a text from Maddy. *The kidnap victim will call at 6 pm tonight.* Great! Now, to clear her head and make a list of questions. She knew she should invite her mother over as well. She'd have questions of her own, for sure.

"Mom, it's me. Maddy set up a phone conversation with the kidnap victim. She's calling Maddy's phone at 6 p.m."

"Oh my God, we're finally going to find Amy."

"Don't get your hopes up. This victim obviously doesn't know where she or the kidnapper is hiding."

"Maybe she overheard them talking about another place. Or…"

"We will see. I'd like to know for sure it was Amy in that cabin. That's my goal."

"I'll be there before 6."

"See you later."

Emily made a list of questions. She wondered if she should invite Megan over as well. As she was working, Megan called.

"Emily, your dresses came in. Can you and Maddy come for a fitting tonight? The shop's open until 7."

"We can't tonight. How about tomorrow?"

"The sooner the better. Kim, the other bridesmaid and I, are going over after work. I'll tell the owner you'll be in tomorrow."

She wondered if she should mention the upcoming call. Nah. She didn't want Megan to feel guilty about not being there, or worse yet, cancel her fitting. "Megan, did you find out if Charlie Adams has an alibi for the day Toby was killed?"

"He doesn't. None of his neighbors saw him. He claims his car was in his garage. He didn't make any phone calls, order pizza…nothing."

"Okay. Good luck with your fitting."

Chapter 10

Staring at the silent phone on the coffee table as if it were a Ouija Board, Emily sat on her hands to prevent them from shaking. Frances drummed her fingers on the table.

"Mom, stop doing that. You sound like an army of horses."

"Emily, this could be it. This phone call may change our lives."

"Don't get your hopes up too high," said Drew. "Remember, we talked about this."

Ignoring his comment, Frances said, "Maddy, the ringer's on, right?"

"Of course, it is."

"Anyone want coffee?" asked Henry, trying but not succeeding in alleviating the tension that gripped the room.

"No thanks," said Drew.

Frances sighed, "It's 6:01. I'll bet she changed her mind."

Henry said, "Give it a few minutes." All four of them sat silently, waiting for Maddy's phone to ring.

"It's 6:03 already. She's not going to call," said Frances. She got up and paced around the living room.

"If she doesn't, we're no worse off than we were," said Emily. Her heart beat inside her chest like a wild animal ready to break free of its cage. She didn't know how much longer she could stand this. She'd prayed this phone call would be productive. Now, she wondered if the victim had chickened out, or worse yet, never intended to call.

"6:06," said Frances. Just then, Maddy's ringtone lit up the room. "What do I say? I'm too nervous. Emily, you talk first."

Maddy put the phone on speaker.

"Hello. I'm calling for Maddy."

Emily said, "Yes, this is her mother. Maddy's Mother. I'm here, and so is my mother, Frances. I have you on speaker."

"If my identity gets out, I could be in great danger. I'm not sure I should be talking to you. This is a mistake."

"No! Please!" said Emily. "I swear we won't let out that we talked to you. Besides, we don't know who or where you are. My sister might be alive after all these years and you're the only link we have."

"I don't know much. I was only there a couple of days."

"I know," said Emily. "Can you describe the woman in the cabin?"

"She was maybe in her forties, had a big face, blond hair."

"And a birthmark, right?" added Frances.

"I thought maybe it was a scar but could have been a birthmark. It looked like a boxing glove."

"On which hand?" said Emily.

"Her left. And not to be mean, but I think she had a mental condition. She spoke kind of funny."

"Did she seem scared?" said Frances.

"Not at all. She was quite pleasant. She was always singing."

Emily's heart squeezed. Amy loved singing, especially in the shower. Emily yelled at her regularly for waking her up in the morning with her crooning. If only she could hear that voice again.

"What else can you tell us?" asked Frances.

"She loved doing dishes. She jumped up as soon as the meals were done and did them by hand. She sang the same song over and over again."

"What song?" asked Frances, clutching her hands together so hard they were turning pale.

"Something about washing her hair."

Frances jumped up. "Gonna wash that man right out of my hair? She loved *South Pacific*. Must have watched the movie a hundred times at least. She sang that song whenever she took a bath or was around water."

"That was it. First I wondered if she meant the kidnapper, but she seemed at ease with him."

"Oh my God. She…she's alive!" said Frances.

Emily felt stunned. Old visions ran through her head—she and Amy playing on the swings, she and Amy playing dolls, she and Amy at the river…What if she wasn't responsible for her death after all?

Frances said, "Do you have any idea where they could have gone after the cabin burned down.?"

"I didn't know it had burned down. I didn't know they'd gone anywhere."

"How did you get away?" asked Emily.

"I was locked in a bedroom. He let me out to eat meals at the table with them. One night, the kidnapper fell asleep. I heard him snoring on the sofa through my door. I heard your sister sweeping outside my door and I whispered to her. Said I felt sick and needed to get some juice. She let me out of the room. Then I said I felt like I was going to throw up. Could she open the door and let me get some air?"

"And she did it?" asked Frances. "She didn't have a mean bone in her body."

"She said sure. I told her I was about to toss my cookies and she should go inside so she didn't have to smell it."

"And she went inside?" said Emily.

"Had to explain I didn't literally mean cookies, but yep. And I ran off into the woods. I was so scared he'd follow me but I guess he didn't wake up right away. I wandered through the woods all night and eventually found a road. A truck driver picked me up and took me to the police station."

"Thank goodness you got away," said Emily. How could she not have seen this man abduct Amy all those years ago? It was still her fault. If she hadn't been distracted by her friends...if she'd paid attention...

Frances said, "How did he abduct you in the first place?"

"I was picking cherries by the river. It was getting dark and I started for home. He snuck up so quiet I never heard him. He put a cloth over my mouth and it smelled really bad, like bleach or something. Next thing I know, I wake up on a metal bed in a room with wooden walls. The door is locked. I pound on it till he comes in and...It's hard to relive this."

"Take your time," said Emily.

"He came into the room. Gave me a glass of water. Said relax, that he'd be sure I'd be safe here."

"Safe?" said Emily.

"I know, weird comment, right? He thought we were being attacked or something. He wore camouflage and had this bushy, gray beard. Wore a green cap. I told the police all this."

"I know, but they won't tell us anything. If there's any clue as to where my daughter is, I have to know. Can you tell us anything else?"

"He had metal shelves all over the kitchen stocked with supplies. Cereals, boxes of granola bars, matches, candles...he was crazy as a loon. Oh, and your sister called him Poppy."

"Did he have a car?"

"No, not that I saw anyway."

Emily said, "What did he call her?" She prayed she'd say Amy—further confirmation she wasn't dreaming.

"He called her Non-young."

"Non-young? What's that mean? She's old now?"

"Weird, right? I have no idea, but she smiled whenever he said it. I've got to go."

Emily said, "Thank you so much."

"Yes, Yes," said Frances. "This is life changing. Please if you remember anything else..."

"I've got your number."

As soon as the call ended, Frances hugged Emily, tears in her eyes. "She's alive! I can't believe it after all these years."

Emily said, "Why didn't she come back to us? Even if she was taken against her will, I'm sure she had the opportunity sometime in the last thirty years to escape."

"Stockholm Syndrome," said Maddy. "I saw it in a movie. Amy bonded with her captor."

Henry said, "And there's no telling what the kidnapper told her. Sounds like she was gullible."

Frances said, "Gullible? She wasn't...isn't...stupid."

"I didn't mean she was. I'm just saying, from what I know about Down's Syndrome, she may have been easy to convince."

Drew said, "That's great, knowing she's alive, but now what? We don't know where she is."

"Emily, you have to get hypnotized. Please."

"Mom, I don't feel comfortable. I don't believe in it."

Maddy said, "It's not like they can make you do anything you wouldn't do. That nonsense about making people bark like a dog or jump into a fire isn't true."

"I know, but…okay. I'll think about it."

"Emily made banana bread. Any takers?" said Henry.

Chapter 11

Emily stared at the ceiling all night thinking about Amy. She was now convinced she was still alive—or at least she was alive when the kidnapping victim escaped. All these years she was sure Amy had drowned. It seemed to be the only logical explanation for her disappearance.

No one was around except for her own two friends and she was talking to them the whole time so they couldn't have taken Amy. Amy's cap floating on the river... If Amy had fallen in, would it have still been visible? With an upcoming storm brewing, the current was even stronger than usual. By the time she saw it, the cap should have been carried away, right?

She was so stupid not to have realized that thirty years ago. If they had gotten a quicker start searching for her in the woods, then maybe...And there had to have been a car parked nearby. The abductor had to have shown his face. Hypnosis? Maybe she owed it to her mother to give it a try. The alarm went off.

Henry rolled over. "Did you sleep at all?"

"No. I shouldn't have jumped to the conclusion that Amy drowned. If we'd searched the woods..."

"Don't go there. Concentrate on finding her now."

"Do you think I should be hypnotized?"

"I can't tell you what to do. How do you feel about it?"

"Like I have no choice. Do you have any recommendations from the hospital?"

"I'm sure I can find someone qualified."

Emily's phone buzzed. "It's a text from Megan. She wants me to meet her at the bridal shop this morning. The wedding will be here before you know it."

Henry said, "Are we going to Toby's funeral tomorrow? We didn't know him, but you've gotten to know Lisa."

"We should show our support. Poor woman. The daughter's suffering too. Her husband should have come with her."

"Why didn't he?"

"Apparently he and Toby didn't get along."

"I've got to get into the shower."

Emily opened her laptop. She was too tired to run this morning, but maybe she could accomplish some writing before meeting Megan.

When Henry finished getting ready, he gave her a kiss and set off for the hospital. He'd start asking around about therapists before the day got too crazy. Emily had been carrying this dark weight ever since he met her—guilt over not watching her sister, guilt over her death. How great would it be to find her now?

"Hey, buddy. Can we go get fitted for our tuxes today?" Pat pulled into the hospital parking lot at the same time as Henry.

"Yeah. You're running outta time. Am I supposed to do one of those bachelor parties for you? It just occurred to me."

"I'm too old for that. If a half-naked woman jumps out of a cake I might have a heart attack or something."

"Did you book a honeymoon?"

"Yes, but it's top secret."

"Okay, if you want to be like that."

"Hawaii. Two weeks soaking up the sunshine, waves breaking on the beach...I can't wait."

"You deserve it, buddy. By the way, do you know the name of a good therapist?"

"I thought you were handling the teenage thing? Is Maddy still trying to get in touch with her inmate father?"

"No, it's not about Maddy. Emily wants to try hypnosis. We spoke to the kidnapping victim last night and we're convinced Amy is alive. Emily wants to try and remember any clues she might have missed."

"From thirty years ago?"

"Her mother's been pressuring her."

"Yeah. The psychiatrist I went to after my wife died was very good. I'll text you her info."

"One more thing. Do you know a chiropractor in town by the name of Willis?"

"Lansford? He's a joke. He works hand in hand with that shady lawyer you see all over TV. The one who promises to win you a bundle if you're in an accident. An ambulance chaser at best."

"The law suit that was going on. Charlie Adams came here to the hospital after he was injured, but I looked up the medical records and it didn't seem like he had any major injuries. The report from the chiropractor tells a different story."

"Sounds about right. I know someone who did that very thing. My next door neighbor. He was hit from behind going really slow. Had not a scratch on him. Then he went to Dr. Lansford who diagnosed him with disc problems, dizzy spells, you name it. Won himself a small fortune."

"So if Charlie's lawsuit was a trumped up hoax and Toby found out about it he'd have been in deep trouble with the law, right?"

"I think that's a hard thing to prove, but I suppose so." Pat pushed the silver button opening the glass door to the emergency entrance.

"Emily said Lisa Cutler told her Toby had received a threatening note that said, *You will pay* in red letters with a skull and crossbones. Pay money? If Toby found out about the scam, turned the tables, and was blackmailing Charlie…"

"Charlie would have benefited from his death, although he'd be out the small fortune he'd have gotten by winning the law suit."

"Didn't Megan say Charlie didn't have an alibi?"

"I think she said that. Hey, I'd better head downstairs. Maybe we can run over to the Formalwear store over lunch if we can coordinate our times."

"Sounds good."

***

When Emily got to the bridal shop, Megan was already there.

"Emily, thanks for meeting me here. The veil I ordered won't be here in time and I have to pick out a replacement."

"Can't you get the floor model? Is that what they call it?"

"I don't want to wear a veil that's been touched and tried on by dozens of other brides-to-be."

"I understand. Let's find you a replacement." She started going through the racks.

The owner came by. "I separated the ones that are possible to get in time for the wedding. They're over here." She led them to a rack. "Let me know if I can help with anything."

"Thanks." Megan shuffled through the choices. "None of these are as good as the original."

"You have to try them on to tell." Emily searched. "This one is pretty. I'll put it aside. And here's one that's similar to the original you showed us."

Megan went to the mirror and started trying them.

"Did you ever get the threatening note back from the crime lab?"

"Yes, but no prints. It was written with a red dry-erase marker. I'm afraid that's all we got."

"Dry-erase marker? Like you use on a white board? Can you get a warrant and search Charlie's house for one?"

"I doubt I could convince a judge to get a warrant. Those markers are everywhere," said Megan.

"No, they aren't. I don't happen to have any laying around the house. Maybe if you have kids you might. Charlie was a custodian. Why would he have dry-erase markers lying around?"

"I have a dry erase board and marker right on my fridge to note when I run out of items. We have no physical evidence linking Charlie to the crime scene. You know what else we don't have?"

"What?"

"Alternate suspects, viable motives—I'm overlooking something." She placed one of the veils on her head and looked in the mirror. "Nah. Can you hand me another one?"

The shop owner emerged from the dressing rooms. "I've got one I think will look beautiful on you." She reached behind the counter and pulled out a lacy veil with a beaded tiara. "The bride-to-be who ordered this one canceled the wedding at the last minute. She didn't even want to pick it up." Megan tried it.

"Megan, that's the one," said Emily.

"Will it go with my dress?"

The shop owner said, "It's perfect with your dress. I'll even give you a discount since you weren't able to get your first choice."

"I'll take it."

The shop owner said, "I'll steam it for you and you can pick it up tomorrow. Did they figure out what happened to the man who fell from the roof yet?"

"I can't discuss an ongoing case. We're working on it."

"Poor old Charlie. There are rumors he's being arrested for the murder. You know that's not possible. Charlie'd never do that to his good friend."

"His good friend?" said Emily.

"Yeah. See the café across the street?" She pointed out the window. "I eat lunch there a lot since it's so close to the shop and all. Anyhow, the post office is just around the corner. Charlie and poor Toby, may he rest in peace, used to eat lunch there, too."

"Together?" said Megan. "Like they were friends?"

"Oh yeah. Then Toby got that job at the school, and Charlie got fired. Only saw them a few times after that."

"They ate lunch together after Charlie fell and started the lawsuit? They must have been discussing business."

"Not the way they were laughing and all."

"Are you sure?"

"Of course I am. I know friendship when I see it."

"You'll call when my dress comes in?" said Megan.

"Of course. It may even come in tomorrow and you can get your final fitting when you pick up the veil."

"Great. It'll save me a trip," said Megan. Emily followed her out the door.

"I've got to get back to work. Thanks for meeting me. I'll talk to you soon."

Emily wondered if another trip to Lisa Cutler's might be in order. Why did she pretend the two of them didn't even know each other except for the law suit? And she denied that he had a high school buddy living here when her daughter swore he did. Something smelled fishy and she wanted to follow her nose to find the source.

Chapter 12

Shari Townshend, looking more pregnant than yesterday, answered the Cutler's door. A tall, clean-shaven gentleman stood behind her and introduced himself.

"I'm Paul, Shari's husband and Lisa's son-in-law." He reached out with an iron handshake.

"I'm sorry for your loss," said Emily. She followed them to the sofa. "I'm sure both your wife and Lisa are glad for the extra hand. Planning a funeral is a lot of work."

"I think we've got all the loose ends tied up at this point. I'm ready to put Toby to rest for good."

"Have you spent much time here in Sugarbury Falls?"

"Nope. First time for me. Shari came out for a few days when her parents first moved here. I had no desire to subject myself to Toby's nonsense."

Shari said, "Paul, are you kidding me? My father's not even cold in the ground and you make a comment like that?"

"Turns out I was right about him. You told me to trust him—go ahead and invest. What a con artist."

Emily was beginning to feel uncomfortable, but her curiosity got the better of her. "What happened, if you don't mind me asking?"

Paul jumped right in. "Toby had a plan. A grandiose, fool-proof investment. What a fool."

Shari interrupted. "Don't speak poorly of my father, Paul."

"Me. I was the fool. I'll leave it at that."

Lisa slumped into the room. "I thought I heard company." She wore the same faded sweats she had on when Emily visited yesterday. Not that clothes were a priority right now.

"Can I get you something to drink?"

"No, I'm not staying long. Yesterday you told me Toby and Charlie hadn't met each other before the accident."

"That's correct."

"I was just over at the bridal shop and the owner claims Toby and Charlie often ate lunch at the café across the street. She's under the impression they were friends."

"She's mistaken. The only thing that brought those two together was the law suit. Period."

Emily turned to Shari. "Didn't you say your father had a high school friend who lived here? We looked at the team picture...there was a Charlie who signed it."

"Mom says no, so I guess it was someone else, or maybe I misunderstood. Mom needs her rest."

"Okay. I'll be going. I'll see you at the funeral tomorrow."

She was almost back to her car when she realized she'd left her phone on Lisa's coffee table. At the front door, she heard Shari and Paul arguing.

Shari screamed, "How dare you! You were going to tell a complete stranger what my father did."

"I have no desire to protect his reputation. I don't care if he is dead. You know what he did to us, right? That was our entire savings."

"You didn't have to be so gullible. Why didn't you check it out before you wrote the check?"

"Can you say *maternity leave*? One less paycheck at best. And my company with its downsizing and layoffs? What if I lost my job? It sounded like the answer to our problem."

"You're an idiot. Dad would have made good on it, especially if he had won the lawsuit, which he was sure he would have. Now that he's dead, that's out the window."

"At least you inherit the condo in San Francisco. We can sell it and recoup some of what we lost."

If she didn't need her phone so badly, she would have left. Emily waited for a break in the shouting match, then knocked. Loudly.

Paul ripped open the door. "What? I thought you'd left."

"Um, I...I'm sorry. I forgot my phone."

Paul flung the door open wider and with an exaggerated gesture said, "Come on in."

She hustled into the living room and avoiding eye contact with Shari, grabbed the phone and left. Wow. Sounds like Paul invested their entire savings in something Toby recommended and now they'd lost everything. With a baby on the way, to boot. If that wasn't a motive for murder, what was? A condo in San Francisco must be worth a pretty penny.

Then again, Paul just got to town yesterday, meaning he may have had motive, but not opportunity. And Toby was Lisa's father. Even if he hated Toby, would he hurt his wife by killing her father? And why on Earth was Lisa lying about Toby and Charlie knowing each other before the lawsuit started?

When she got home, she was surprised to see Jessica and Sam in the living room with Henry and Maddy. As soon as they saw her, the room fell silent.

"Did I interrupt something?" She looked from Henry to Maddy.

Maddy said, "You might as well tell her."

"Tell me what?"

Henry said, "Sit down. Maddy has something to tell you."

"Now, you're worrying me," said Emily.

Maddy said, "Henry forbid me to talk to my father and I don't think it's fair."

Emily said, "What are you talking about? Of course you can't mean the father who's in prison."

"He's still my father."

Emily sighed. "We talked about this when I caught you answering his letters a while back."

"I have a right to know my father."

Jessica said, "I was explaining to Maddy that our father broke the law and deceived dozens of unsuspecting patients. She needs to stay clear."

"I caught her telling him she loved him over the phone," said Henry.

"And you didn't tell me? When was this?" Emily felt her blood pressure rise.

"Just a few days ago. You have so much on your mind with Amy and the wedding."

"I'm her mother. I have a right to know."

"And I'm her father I…"

"You're not my father!" said Maddy. "And how come my calls aren't going through to the prison anymore? You blocked them, didn't you!"

"Anymore?" said Emily.

Henry said, "I called Jessica to try and talk some sense into her sister. She agrees with me, as I'm sure you do, that any contact with her father is a bad idea. And yes. I called the phone company and blocked your calls. Did you know they have an app for that?"

Jessica said, "Maddy, you are so lucky to have two parents who love you and care so much. My mother was a single mother. I never got to have a father like Henry, yet I never want to see that monster sperm donor face to face."

Sam said, "Once you start with the calls, you have no idea what'll happen. Your father, I mean the prisoner, could potentially send your personal information into cyberspace. It's a dangerous world."

"F you," said Maddy.

"Are you kidding? You know we don't allow that sort of language in this house," said Henry.

Maddy said, "As soon as I turn 18, I'm out of here. Three and a half years and you'll never see me again." She grabbed Chester off the back of the sofa and stomped back to her room.

Henry said, "Wait for it…"

Right on cue, the door slammed so hard the floor shook.

Jessica said, "She'll come around. You have to stand firm. She's the child, you're the parents."

"Apparently Maddy doesn't consider me a parent," said Henry.

"They get that way when they're teenagers," said Sam. "One minute they're slamming doors, and the next, they're asking for money. Just kidding. The bond between a father and daughter is complicated but there's nothing like it."

Emily said, "I didn't know you had a daughter."

Sam said, "Um, I, well, I don't. Not anymore."

Jessica said, "Sam, you said you were divorced, but never told me you had a child. I'm so sorry."

"I don't want to talk about it. Can we go?"

"Sure. Henry, she'll get over it. And you and Emily are doing a fantastic job; don't let what she said make you doubt yourself."

"Thanks. I'm surprised at how much she's getting to me. It's usually Emily she goes after." He smiled. Emily tossed a throw pillow at him. He locked the door behind them.

"This day couldn't get much worse," said Emily. Her phone vibrated.

"Emily, it's Mom. I found us a hypnotist!"

Chapter 13

The charcoal sky hovered over the church. On the way to the funeral, it had been sprinkling on and off, but standing at the church entrance, Emily knew it was a matter of time before the storm broke.

"Let's go in and get a seat," said Henry. He grabbed a program. "Looks like we have our pick of spots."

"He didn't live here long. Not enough time to make a church full of friends, anyway," said Emily.

Lisa Cutler, her daughter Shari, and son-in-law Paul occupied the front pew. Across the aisle, were Jessica, Sam, and—Emily guessed—colleagues from the school where Toby had recently started working as a security guard. Emily looked over her shoulder.

"Henry, isn't that Charlie Adams from the bar? That must be his wife next to him."

Although he'd taken a seat in the back corner of the church, Emily spotted him right away. She half wondered if he'd come to the funeral, given what the bridal shop owner told her about how he and Toby ate lunch together frequently.

"That's him. Isn't it kind of strange? I mean, the deceased was suing him and all," said Henry.

"I guess he just wants to pay his respects. Besides, I doubt there was as much animosity between them as you'd expect, given the pending law suit."

A solo soprano began to sing, and the priest took his place. Emily's mind wandered throughout the service. She couldn't believe she'd agree to be hypnotized, but her mother wouldn't let up. Secretly, Emily hoped she would remember something that might lead them to Amy. Henry nudged her and she realized everyone was kneeling. He nudged her again when it was time to sit back on the pew.

Lisa Cutler wiped her nose and dabbed at her eyes with a white handkerchief throughout the service. Shari buried her head in her hands. Paul periodically put his arm around his wife, but mostly sat erect with his arms folded across his chest.

Emily heard thunder. By the time the mass ended and they followed the casket to the front, it was out and out pouring. Lisa made an announcement.

"Please join us," she began sobbing. "Come back to our…"

Paul took over. "You are all invited back to the house for food and to honor my father-in-law's life."

Jessica and Sam came over. Always prepared, Jessica had brought a golf umbrella with her. Emily struggled to open the portable umbrella she'd shoved into her purse at the last minute.

Henry said, "Did the two of you know him well?"

Jessica said, "I'd gotten to know him a little. Whenever I stayed late at school, he stayed at the door and watched to make sure I got to my car."

Sam said, "He would have sucked in a crisis. He was all about being friends with the students. Dollars to donuts he'd run the other way if there was a real emergency."

"That's an awful thing to say," said Jessica. "If you didn't like him, why did you show up here?"

"It would have looked bad if I didn't. The principal was sitting right behind us and you know she noticed who was there."

"You should have cleaned up better," said Jessica.

"My shirt's clean and so is my blazer."

"But what's on your hand, paint?"

He licked his finger and scrubbed it. "It's not paint. That's what happens when you come straight from school."

"You're such a slob," said Jessica.

Emily noticed Lisa huddled in a corner. "Excuse me, I'll be right back."

Lisa's back was to her. She was talking to Charlie Adams. Not wanting to interrupt, Emily hung back under the ledge.

"Now what? We had this all worked out and it blew up in our faces."

"Believe me, I'm not happy either. I lost my job over the whole fiasco. It would have worked if…"

"If my husband hadn't been murdered?"

"Yeah. Now we're both in deep water without a paddle."

"It's going to hurt Shari and Paul. They're about to have a family to feed. Toby was going to use the money to pay back them back."

"I'd come back to the house, but it might be inappropriate."

"Yeah. People will wonder. Your wife is getting wet standing in the parking lot. You should go." She gave him a prolonged hug.

Emily gave it a minute, then came out from the ledge. "Lisa, it was a beautiful service. Do you need me to pick up anything at the grocery store on the way to your house?"

"No. It's under control." She joined her daughter and Paul.

Emily went back to her family. "Ready to go?"

Henry said, "Yes. How's Lisa? I mean, I know she can't be great."

"She was talking to Charlie Adams. She said she'd never heard of him before the law suit, yet it seemed like they were old friends just a few minutes ago. Or more."

"Or more?" questioned Henry.

"It sounded like they may be, you know, involved with each other."

"He's got a wife right? Never mind. Just because I find it immoral, doesn't mean everyone does."

"What if Charlie killed Toby so he and Lisa could be together?"

"He was probably being polite. I'm surprised he came at all."

"That's what I mean. There's more going on than meets the eye."

"Sounds like your imagination may be taking liberties. All you saw was a hug. Let's head over to the Cutler house and out of this rain."

When they got to the house, it was raining even harder. Emily didn't bother with her tiny umbrella; she made a run for the overhang. While she waited for Henry and Maddy, she smelled lasagna and garlic bread through the door.

"Isn't it open?" said Henry. He turned the knob. No point standing out here in the rain.

Coralee and Noah were setting up food on the kitchen counter. Coralee said, "How was the service?"

"I forgot you were catering this," said Emily.

"Paul Townshend asked if I'd do it. He fell in love with my food when he was in town."

"He just got here. When did he have a chance to eat at the inn?"

"Last week. He was only here one night. Said he had business in town."

"What kind of business?"

"I didn't ask."

"Which night was it?" asked Emily.

"Let's see...it was Friday night. He checked out Saturday."

"That's the night before Toby was killed," said Emily. "He didn't mention he'd been in town. And why wouldn't he have stayed with Lisa and Toby?"

"It's not my business," said Coralee. "I've got to get this food set out. People are arriving already."

A new piece to the puzzle. This didn't make any sense. Shari mentioned Paul and Toby didn't get along, and it was Toby's fault Paul was nearly bankrupt.

Henry said, "Lisa, Paul, and Shari just arrived. Let's go offer our condolences, get a quick bite to eat, and go home."

Paul and Shari went for plates just as Coralee was bringing out a pan of food. Paul quickly turned around, as if to avoid her. *He's afraid she'll spill the beans to Shari that he was in town the day of the murder.*

Emily recognized a few of the guys from the bar. They were toasting Toby.

"Raise our glasses, or should I say grasses, to Toby, may he rest in peace."

"Here, here." They clinked glasses.

One of the men said, "Grasses. Good one. I'll miss that lisp of his."

"It ain't a lisp he had. He sounded like he was Chinese or something."

"Don't go being disrespectful now."

"Disrespectful? Toby joked about it all the time."

"I meant don't go being disrespectful to the Chinese," said one of the men. They all laughed.

A speech impediment? Then it was Toby she heard being bullied at the fair when she stopped to tie her shoe. She thought there may have been a connection, but now she knew for sure. If only she knew who was yelling at him and making those threats... *I'll bet they resumed the argument up on the roof.*

"Emily, I want to get home. Ready?"
"Yes. Let's say our goodbyes and get out of here."

Chapter 14

"What kind of therapist has hours on a Saturday?" said Emily. She, Henry, and Frances waited on a faded sofa in the psychiatrist's waiting room. "The building is locked. She had to give us a code just to get in. And we drove an hour, worried about being on time, now we have to wait?"

"You're doing this for your sister," said Frances. "If you have a bad attitude going in it's not going to work."

"A bad attitude? What is it, like a séance? If I send out bad vibes, the spirits won't appear?"

Henry said, "Calm down. We're here now. If it doesn't work, you can at least say you tried." The door flew open, and a young woman wearing glasses opened the door.

I'll bet the glasses are for show. She looks like she's twelve. She extended her hand. "I'm Emily Fox. This is my husband and my mother."

"Come in and have a seat. Your mother explained over the phone what you hope to achieve. Under hypnosis, you may remember something you saw that day to help you find your sister."

"Right off the bat, you should know I'm not hypnotizable."

Frances said, "Everyone can be hypnotized, isn't that right, doctor?"

"Not everyone. I've had patients who were resistant to hypnosis."

Frances said, "Emily wants to find her sister so she isn't going to resist, isn't that right?" She looked directly at her daughter. Emily felt like getting up and leaving right then and there.

The doctor seemed to sense the tension and didn't give Emily a chance to answer. "Relax and let's give it a shot. Nothing ventured, nothing gained. Have a seat in the recliner." She turned down the lights and spoke softly. "Think about a peaceful place. It may be a beach, or a spot in the woods, or your own bathtub surrounded by bubbles. Picture the sounds, picture your body letting go."

Emily took slow, breaths and pictured herself at the beach. *This is stupid. The sand is too hot and I left my sunscreen home.*

"Relax your feet, now your legs, now your arms..." Not wanting to be labeled resistant, she tried to cooperate. Emily followed the instructions, feeling her body sink into the chair.

"You're in the woods, on the bank of a river. Your sister is there with you. Picture it. She paused. What was she wearing? Could you hear the water rushing, or feel the sun on your skin? Don't answer, just imagine."

Emily visualized her sister, dressed in overalls with a pink t-shirt underneath. She'd braided Amy's hair that morning. The current was strong—she heard the water as it rushed over rocks.

"Who else is there with you? Friends? Picture them. What are you doing? Where's Amy?"

She heard a noisy engine and pictured her two friends, getting out of an old Chevette. Amy picked cherries; she was close to the bank, but disappeared behind a large tree. Emily's friend chattered on about the boy she was crushing on. Her friend heard that he wanted to ask her out...

"You're doing great, Emily. Keep visualizing. What's happening?"

"I'm giggling with my friends. I feel the wind picking up. They get back into the car and drive away. I pick up the empty pail next to my feet. I look for Amy."

"Do you see your sister?"

"No. I call her name. I see movement behind the oak tree and hear rustling. I call out to Amy. Then, I see her cap, floating in the river. I wonder why it's not moving, then see it's caught on a rock. Amy's pail of cherries toppled over. The cherries are all over the ground."

"Is anyone else there? Do you hear something, smell something?"

"Wait. I do. I'm following the river, looking for Amy and I see movement out of the corner of my eye. I hear something, but I can't identify it."

"Is it your sister?"

"No. It's a man. He's big. At first I think it's a bear. It's a man, dressed in green. He blended in with the trees. I hear something. In a moment he's gone."

"Does he have Amy?"

"I don't know. I can't see."

"What else do you see?"

"Nothing. He's gone. I'm looking for Amy. I run back to the house." She felt her muscles tense. "I can't find her. She's gone."

"Okay. I'm going to count backwards. When you wake up, you'll feel refreshed and remember everything you said. Three, two, one."

When Emily woke up, she did remember the entire session. It wasn't like being asleep, it was like when you're in bed thinking about sleep but not quite there. When she looked at the time, thirty minutes had passed. She felt like it had been five minutes.

Frances said, "Well? What did the man look like? What did you hear?"

The therapist said, "Let her relax. She did great."

Henry said, "You know the man took her and it sounds like the same man who took the victim. They both wore camouflage, right?"

"Yes. I'm sure there was a man in army green who looked like a bear. He had something on him. On his shoulder."

"Like a patch or a medal?"

"No. It was bigger I can't see it."

The therapist said, "It will come to you when you're relaxed and not thinking about it. Just for the record, you are definitively hypnotizable. It wasn't as bad as you thought, was it?"

"No, not at all. Thank you."

When they got into the car, the badgering started. Frances fired questions like a woodpecker attacking a tree.

"Did the man have a tattoo? Did you hear his voice? Did you hear a car pull away?"

"Mom, stop. That's enough for today. She said if I relax I might remember more. You aren't helping."

Drew said, "Now you know it was the same kidnapper. Sounds just like what the woman on the phone told you, right?"

"Yes. I'm sure it was him. Only, we aren't any further along in finding her. I saw nothing leading us to Amy."

Henry said, "I'm going to drop the two of you off at the inn and take Emily back home to rest. It's been a stressful morning."

Emily closed her eyes, pretending to sleep, until they pulled in front of Coralee's.

Frances said, "If you remember anything, write it down and call me."

Emily opened her eyes. "Yes, I will do that."

Drew said, "We'll touch base later." He helped Frances out of the car and walked her toward the inn.

Henry said, "Peace, at last. You okay?"

"Yeah. I don't want to dwell on this. I'm disappointed I didn't see anything more helpful and the more I stress over it..."

"The less likely you'll remember. You should relax this afternoon."

Sensing vulnerability, Emily said, "I have a great idea. How about we ride out to the animal shelter and look at dogs. I've been wanting a running companion."

"I never agreed to a dog."

"I'm not saying we have to get one. Let's just look at them. It'll take my mind off things. We have to pick up Maddy first. She'd kill us if we went visiting dogs without her."

Thinking this might be the bridge to repairing his recently stressed relationship with Maddy, he agreed. "We're just going to look, right?"

"Yes. I'll call Maddy." He punched in her number. "Maddy, can you be ready to go out in a few minutes?"

"Why? Where are we going?"

"We're going to ride over to the shelter and look at dogs."

"Really? We're getting a dog? I can't believe it. What kind of dog?"

"We're not getting a dog, we're just browsing. Emily is considering getting a running companion. Dogs are a lot of work, especially if they aren't house broken."

When they got to their house, Maddy jumped into the Jeep. "I can't believe we're getting a dog."

Henry said, "We're looking at dogs. I told you I haven't made up my mind. It's a big commitment and we have a cat to consider. I'm not walking a dog in the middle of the night in the freezing cold of winter."

Maddy said, "I'll walk it."

Still relatively new to the parenthood experience, Henry believed her. Besides, Emily wanted a running companion so between the two of them, walks would be covered. He wouldn't be responsible for more than the occasional vet bill.

Maddy said, "There's a shelter right outside of town. They have all types of animals. There's a Grey Hound rescue not far from here. They're good running companions."

"Since we're not sure what type of dog we're looking for, let's start with the shelter," said Emily.

The shelter was a freestanding building which looked like a warehouse from the road. When they entered, they were given paperwork to fill out before getting a tour.

"I'll take you to the dog area. Write down the cage number of those you're interested in. Do you have a particular type of dog in mind?"

"No," said Emily. "I was considering a running companion." They followed, passing smaller dogs and a cat room on the way.

Henry interjected, "We're just looking. We haven't decided to get one. Just exploring options."

"I understand. My name is Shayla. I'll be up front if you have any questions."

They started at the back of the facility.

"They look so sad," said Maddy. She reached through the wires and called to a skinny, black and brown mutt. He hobbled over and licked her fingers.

Emily found two beagles lying in a cage. "They look too tired to be running companions."

Maddy said, "That's because they're depressed. Wouldn't you be?"

Henry said, "They look like brothers. It'd be wrong to split them up." He saw Maddy's mouth open and headed her off. "No, I wouldn't consider getting two dogs. I'm not convinced I want one."

They passed a cage with what looked like a lab mix. A family was already engaged with him. Henry noticed the father writing down the dog's information. He heard a whimper from the far end of the row and followed it. In the cage, sat a really ugly dog! He hobbled over to the front of the cage and whimpered until Henry came closer. "What's wrong, boy?"

The dog stuck a paw through the cage and looked at Henry with the biggest, saddest eyes. Henry stuck his fingers in and scratched the dog between the ears. The dog, some sort of boxer, pit bull, terrier kind of mix, licked his finger. Henry noticed he was missing a leg.

"What's wrong, boy? How did that happen?"

The dog, he swore, tried to answer him. He vocalized the way Chester engaged in meowing conversations with Maddy. Then his tail wagged and Henry was sure he saw a smile. Did dogs actually smile?

"Henry, where are you?" called Emily.

"I'm coming." He started to walk away, but the dog whimpered so sadly, Henry had to turn around.

"It's okay, boy. Someone will adopt you soon." He again walked away to the sound of whimpering. It was an effort not to turn back around.

Maddy said, "There's a lab mix that looks friendly. He's only two years old and I'll bet he'd be a good running companion," said Maddy. "Come see."

"I'll be right there." Henry heard the dog bark a weak bark. He went back and read the dog's information. Sam was five years old and lost his leg when he was trapped in a bear trap. He'd been at the shelter for over a year. Henry went to find Shayla.

"Did you find dog you're interested in?" asked Shayla.

"Um, I just had a few questions. About Sam. The three-legged dog."

"Poor Sam. He's been here over a year and it's doubtful he'll find a home. He has the sweetest personality, but he's very shy and doesn't take to people. That coupled with his injury and the fact that he's neither a puppy nor a fluffy little fur ball, works against him."

"I'm imagining he wouldn't be much of a running companion."

"You'd be surprised. Given the opportunity and lots of encouragement, you never know."

"I'm guessing a three-legged dog would be hard to care for."

"Not really. You have to make sure they don't put too much pressure on the elbow joint from leaning. Keep his weight down but don't over-exercise. Keep the nails trimmed to help with balance. Are you interested in playing with Sam?"

"I don't know. We have a cat at home."

"We do cat tests when they first come in. As I remember, he wasn't aggressive at all, but I'll check the file."

"It's him I'd be worried about in my house!"

Shayla laughed, though Henry hadn't meant to be funny. Chester could be a little possessive.

"I'll set you up in a room. Go get your wife and daughter and just see what you think." She ran off before Henry could object. She'd barely made it around the corner when he heard Emily.

"Henry? Where are you?"

"Coming." Henry found Emily and Maddy. "Come on. We're going to play with a dog."

"What?" said Maddy. "You found us a dog?" Her eyes sparkled.

"I didn't say that. It's just...well, this poor dog wants some attention and he seems to like me."

"Henry, what kind of dog is he?"

"Well, he's not exactly a cute dog. And he only has three legs, so the running thing might be hard."

They settled into the room. Shayla led Sam in on a leash. As soon as she unbuckled it, Sam hobbled over to Henry, licking him and wagging his tail. He didn't seem to notice Emily and Maddy.

"Hey, boy. You're sure an ugly dog, you know."

Sam barked, then somewhat clumsily, laid across Henry's feet and rolled over.

"He wants you to rub his tummy," said Maddy. Henry complied. Whenever he stopped rubbing, Sam whimpered.

Emily said, "He loves you, Henry."

Shayla said, "I've never seen him take to someone like he's taken to your husband."

Maddy and Emily gently pet Sam, who didn't at all mind.

Emily said, "We have a cat. I don't know if they'd get along."

"He does well with cats, but you can take him home to see and if worse comes to worst, bring him back. I figured he was destined to stay here. Not one person all year has shown an interest in him."

Maddy said, "Can we take him home?"

Henry said, "I don't know. Emily wants a running companion. And a three-legged dog is even more work than an able-bodied one."

"Not really," said Shayla. "He won't be jumping up on your sofa or your bed."

"We have a ladder leading up to our bedroom..."

"Please," said Maddy.

Henry's heart couldn't leave this dog behind. "We'll give it a try."

"I'll gather the paperwork," said Shayla. She practically skipped out of the room.

Sam rolled over on Henry's feet as if to keep him from leaving.

"It's okay, boy. Looks like you've found yourself a home. Let's hope Chester doesn't scare you to death."

While the paperwork was processed, and Sam bathed and readied to go to his new home, Emily wandered into the small store area. She had major doubts about this becoming her new running buddy, but he and Henry really had a bond and she and Maddy could fall in love with just about any animal on the planet. She picked out a royal blue leash, a matching collar, and was looking at the ID tags when Maddy came up behind her.

"What are we going to call him? We can't use Sam, that's Jessica's boyfriend's name."

"I think this Sam would treat her better, don't you?"

Maddy giggled. "We should let Henry name him. We can order tags from Amazon after we have a name. We'll need a food bowl and a water bowl." She picked up the choices from the shelf. "I like this one. It's heavy and won't slide around like the plastic ones."

Emily held it. "It's dishwasher safe, too." She looked at the price. It was higher than she imagined it'd be, but a portion of the sales went directly back to the shelter. She picked up a second one for Prancer, then a third for Abby and Rebecca's border collie, Milo.

Henry said, "I got a few things for him." His arms were spilling over with toys and treats.

Maddy said, "So you do have a heart."

Emily placed the bowls on the counter. "What's that supposed to mean?"

Henry cleared his throat. "She didn't think I'd give in and get you a dog."

A loud, creaky voice filled the shop. "Dogs rock. Dogs rock."

Emily jumped and looked up. Behind the cashier in a large cage, a brightly colored parrot had started a monologue.

The cashier said, "That's just Dodo. He's a fixture in this place. Think he was here when they opened thirty years ago. They live forever, you know."

"Birds are best. Birds are best," said the parrot.

"Calm down, Dodo," said the cashier. "Dogs are best."

"Dogs are best. Dogs are best."

Emily froze. That was it.

"Are you okay?" said Henry.

"That sound. The tone, not the words. That's what I heard. When I was at the river with Amy. I saw something on the army man's shoulder under hypnosis. That's it!"

Maddy said, "What's it? A parrot?"

"The man who abducted Amy had a parrot on his shoulder."

Henry said, "Like a patch, or a tattoo?"

"No. A real, live, parrot."

Chapter 15

Henry scooped Sam out of the car and carried him into the house. Emily and Maddy lugged the bags of toys, food, bowls, brush, dog shampoo, flea medicine, and the memory foam dog bed. Maddy called for Chester, but he was hiding somewhere in the house.

Henry said, "This is your new home, Sam. What do you think?"

Sam sniffed the perimeter of the living room, then lifted his leg and peed on the base of the coffee table. Maddy ran for the paper towels, wiping it before Henry could utter a word.

"Do you think he's house broken?" said Emily.

"If that's any indication..."

Maddy said, "Dad, this is a new place. He just has to get used to it."

"I hope you're right." He looked at Emily. "This was your idea."

"I didn't say anything. Maybe we should take him for a walk." Emily grabbed the new leash and attached it. Sam sat down and whimpered. "Come on, Sam. Let's go meet the neighbors." Sam didn't budge.

"Let me try," said Henry. He took the leash from Emily and clicked his tongue against his teeth. "Come on, boy. Let's go for a walk." Sam got up, wagged his tail, and followed Henry to the door. "Come on girls. Looks like we're going for a walk."

Emily grabbed the two extra bowls she'd purchased at the shelter store and locked the door behind them. Sam was a little slow, but able to keep Henry's modified pace. He stopped to sniff every rock and tree along the way, marking most as his territory.

Around the lake, Emily spotted Abby with Milo. She bent down and whispered to him. "Let's go meet a new friend."

When they were nearer, Milo and Sam sniffed each other, both curious, neither aggressive.

"I think they'll be friends," said Abby. "So you decided to get a dog? He's adorable." She bent down to pet Sam. "I thought you wanted a running companion?"

"I did, but Sam took to Henry, or maybe it was the other way around. We couldn't leave him at the shelter."

"I'm hoping he's housebroken," said Henry.

"He's about Milo's size. We have an extra dog crate if you want to borrow it."

"After being locked in a cage for a year, I wouldn't do that to him," said Henry.

"It's like their den. It'll make him feel safe, you'll see. And because they don't like to soil where they sleep, you take him out for a walk after he's been in there and he'll get used to doing his business outdoors."

"I guess we could try it, if he doesn't already know better."

Emily gave one of the bowls to Abby. "Here's a present for Milo. I got it at the shelter store."

Abby took it out of the bag. "Thank you! Milo will love it. Come by the house. Rebecca will be excited to meet Sam."

They followed Abby to her cabin. "Rebecca, there's someone we want you to meet," said Abby. "She must be up in the bedroom. I'll get her."

While she was fetching Rebecca, Emily noticed an array of photos spread out on the table. Abby, being a photographer, must have done a recent shoot.

Abby came downstairs. "She'll be right down."

"Abby, these photos are beautiful."

"The Chamber of Commerce hired me to do a new travel brochure. I've been shooting iconic Sugarbury Falls scenes. Here's Coralee's inn, and the covered bridge. I shot this one at the winter festival."

Emily looked through the rest. "Is this the diner across from the post office?"

"Yeah. It's been here forever and the owner's family has run it since the 1920's."

Emily picked up a photo. "Isn't this Toby Cutler? And it looks like he's eating with Charlie Adams!" In the photo, the two men appeared to be laughing over hash browns and fried eggs.

"Yeah, I remember thinking it was eerie. I'd just taken that the morning before Toby Cutler died."

Emily said, "The morning before he died? These two don't look like opponents in a potentially expensive law suit to me. Something's not adding up. Lisa has a team picture of Charlie and Toby from back in their high school days. I'm sure it has to have been Charlie."

Rebecca came downstairs and made a beeline for Sam. She held out her hand for him to sniff. "He's so ugly he's cute! What's his name?"

"For now, Sam. That's Jessica's boyfriend's name so we'll be changing it."

"Speaking of names," said Emily, "I hate to ask, but can you see if Toby Cutler and Charlie Adams went to school together? Lisa Cutler says no, but I think she's lying."

Rebecca said, "Why would she lie about that?"

"I'm not sure. I think I'll pay her another visit."

"I'll grab my laptop," said Rebecca. "Tell me the names again?"

"Charlie Adams and Toby Cutler."

She tapped on the keys. After a few minutes, she said, "I have Charlie Adams graduating but no Toby Cutler."

"Maybe he was a year older or younger?"

"Sorry, Emily. I don't see any Toby Cutler on this roster. If they knew each other from school, I'm not finding it. Maybe one of them was at a private school."

"This is strange. I guess Lisa Cutler was telling the truth when she said Toby didn't have a high school friend here in town. It doesn't mean that they didn't become friends. The photo Abby took sure makes it look as though they were friends."

Sam tugged on his leash and whined.

Henry said, "He needs to go outside. I think he's housebroken after all."

Abby said, "Congrats on your new family member. Let us know if we can help. We've been dog parents for a long, long time."

Henry led with Sam while Emily and Maddy tried to keep up.

"For a three-legged dog, this boy's fast," said Emily. "Maybe he'll make a good running companion after all."

"We've got to change his name before Jessica meets him." said Maddy. "What should we call him?"

Henry said, "Let's call him Gimp."

"No," said Maddy. "He'll think we're making fun of him."

"I think it's kind of cute," said Emily. "Or how about a nice Scottish name to honor your family, Maddy? Duffy? Angus?"

"Angus is the name of my dead uncle."

"He's sure full of energy," said Henry. Sam pulled ahead after stopping to mark the pine tree as his territory. "Full of Spunk."

"That's it," said Maddy. "Let's call him Spunky." When she said his name, Spunky looked at her and wagged his tail.

"Okay with you, Em?"

"I love it. Spunky it is. Maddy can go online and order a name tag. Do we pay by the letter? If so, maybe we should just call him Bo, or Ty."

"Not funny," said Maddy, but Henry saw her hide a smile.

When they got to the house, Maddy set up the dog bed and ordered the tag while Emily and Henry collapsed on the sofa.

"This day seems like a week," said Emily. "The hypnosis experience was stressful, and then getting a new family member? Hey, did you see Chester? It's only a matter of time before he meets Spunky."

As if on cue, Chester darted out of the kitchen and jumped on Emily's lap. "You'll always be my baby, Chester. Maybe you'll enjoy having a dog to tease."

"I was thinking about what you said at the shelter store. About the parrot."

"Yeah. I'll bet the kidnapper had a parrot on his shoulder the day he grabbed Amy. Only, how didn't I notice? Surely he'd have been squawking the whole time. I should have heard him."

"I don't know anything about parrots. Maybe he was trained to stay quiet. Wait. I know one thing. They have very long lives."

"You're saying this parrot could still be alive? I don't know how that helps us, even if he is."

"Guess you're right. Unless they're registered or go for regular vet visits...I'm not sure what I'm thinking."

"The guy's been living in a cabin in the woods, dressed like a camouflaged bear for the past 30 years or so. What are the odds he seeks veterinary care or that he registered his bird?" Even as she said those words, a spark of hope welled inside her. *Maybe someone out there remembers a weird guy with a parrot and can lead us to him.* She knew this was the very definition of grasping at straws.

"Let's watch some escapist TV. Give me the remote." Henry flicked through the channels. "How about our favorite lawyer show?"

"Okay with me." She snuggled next to him. "It's strange how Rebecca couldn't find Toby's name on the graduating list."

"I thought we were going to give it a rest and watch TV?"

"Okay. I'll shut up." She stared at the screen, getting caught up in the story. As the show progressed, she felt a tingle of familiarity. "Henry, look at this plot. An officer shoots a man she thinks is coming after her in the arm. It turns out he was unarmed. He turns around and sues not only her, but the police department."

"Big bucks at stake."

They continued watching. "Look. The police officer is on the stand. She doesn't even appear to try to defend her actions. She's admitting she didn't get a good look and had been drinking! Look at her lawyer's face!" Emily pointed to the screen.

"There's a client who could have stood for more jury prep if I ever saw one."

"It's like she's throwing the case."

"And setting herself up to lose!"

"What?" said Emily. "They're resting the case? Jury's going to deliberate. How can they possibly find her anything but guilty? She admitted she was ill-trained by the department to handle a split second call like the one she made."

"The police department—the city—has deep pockets. Imagine the payout when they determine she was guilty." Henry shook his head.

"Yes, imagine."

After the commercial, the jury returned, delivering a guilty verdict.

"That's the end of her career," said Henry. The next scene was in a bedroom. The officer and the victim were high fiving, then dove under the covers together.

"Doesn't look like a contemptuous relationship to me!"

"Wait." Henry sat up. "What if our buddy Charlie and his friend Toby saw this episode? Or simply cooked up a similar scheme?"

"Toby pretends to fall on the icy steps, sues Charlie and the city, then they split the profits? Devious."

"At the bar, you thought Charlie was sad about Toby's death."

"And I'm sure it was Toby in the team picture. And the owner of the bridal shop says she saw the two of them eating friendly lunches across the street at the café. Maybe that's why Toby used a false name."

"What about the picture Abby blew up for you? Ice on the steps but not on the sidewalk in front of them? I think we figured it out."

"I'll call Megan," said Emily, reaching for her phone.

"It's late. And in the morning, this might seem far-fetched when we reevaluate. Let's wait."

"I'm up for paying a visit to our grieving widow tomorrow after breakfast. Do you think Charlie killed Toby after all? Maybe he had second thoughts about going through with it and Charlie was afraid they'd be arrested."

"Let's sleep on it." Spunky hobbled in from Maddy's room and stared at Henry, giving a single bark.

"I think he needs to go out," said Emily. "And he wants you to take him. I'm going to bed."

"Thanks, my love. No, I don't need you to come along for a late night walk in the cold."

He grabbed Spunky's leash. "Come on, boy. It's just me and you." He tousled his head and the dog licked him. "I love you too."

Chapter 16

When Emily woke up the next morning, Henry was already out of bed. She'd decided to skip her run so they could get over to Lisa Cutler's place bright and early. She came down the steps just as Henry and Spunky came in the front door.

"Boy, that was one long walk," said Emily. "I go to bed, you're out with the dog; I wake up and you're coming in."

"Very funny. Spunky and I are getting to know each other; isn't that right?"

Spunky barked.

"Watch this. Sit, Spunky." He sat at Henry's feet. "He's a smart dog. Someone took the time to train him. Can't believe he was abandoned like he was."

"Maybe the owner couldn't afford the vet bill after he was injured. At the shelter they said he underwent multiple surgeries after he was rescued from the bear trap."

"Well, he's got a new home now. And Chester doesn't seem phased by him."

Chester was eating his food. When Spunky investigated the pleasure of cat food, Chester darted out of the kitchen.

"No, Spunky!" said Emily. "You were saying?" She picked up the bowl and put it on the counter. "Looks like Chester will be eating up here from now on."

"An elevated dining experience. I'd say that's a win for Chester."

"Ha-ha. Eat your breakfast so we can get over to the Cutlers'."

"Should I wake up Maddy to take care of Spunky?"

"You're kidding, right? Wake her up before noon on a Sunday? She'll hate you."

Henry figured she already hated him right now, since he'd forbidden her to have contact with her convict father. He downed a cup of coffee. "I'm ready when you are."

Emily scribbled a quick note to Maddy and stuck it on the fridge, in case she did wake up. They hopped into Henry's Jeep and drove to the Cutler house, roads pretty much abandoned except for a bit of church traffic as they neared town. Paul's car was in the driveway behind Lisa's. It was a little early, but Emily saw light peeking beneath the living room blinds as they approached the stoop.

Lisa answered. "Emily? Henry?"

"I hope we're not too early."

"I haven't been sleeping. I don't know night from day anymore. Come in."

They sat on the sofa.

"Can I get you coffee or anything? We still have cake leftover from the funeral."

"No thanks." Emily dove right in. "Henry and I were thinking about the lawsuit against Toby. Some details don't add up. For example, it seems as though Charlie and Toby were long-time friends, judging by the picture."

"That's not true."

"Your daughter said Toby had an old friend living here in Sugarbury Falls. Was that friend Charlie?"

"I told you she was mistaken. Multiple times as I remember. What are you getting at?"

Henry said, "Is it possible that Charlie and Toby cooked up a scheme to get money by suing the city? If

Charlie and the post office were negligent in keeping the property safe, Toby stood to gain a big payout."

"One he could have split with Toby," added Emily.

"You're crazy. They'd never met before this happened. And why would he split the money when he could have it all to himself?"

"We know they knew each other. They'd been at Ralph's regularly, drinking and playing pool together. And I saw you talking to Charlie at the funeral," said Emily.

Shari and Paul came into the living room. "Mom, is that true?" said Shari.

"I…no."

Paul said, "Is that how he hoped to make back the fortune he'd lost in that stupid investment? Was that how he was going to pay me back my savings he'd talked me into investing?"

Lisa broke down. "Yes, okay. It's true. They were old school friends. Charlie convinced us to move here. It was the only way out. We were going into bankruptcy. And Shari, we knew you needed money to raise our grandchild."

"That wasn't the way to do it," said Shari.

"When he said he'd pay me back, I had no idea this is what he meant," said Paul. "Is she going to be arrested?"

Henry said, "She didn't actually participate in the plan, right?"

Lisa jumped in. "No. It was all Toby's idea. I swear."

"We have to tell the police but you won't do jail time for simply knowing about your husband's scheme. Charlie on the other hand…" Henry shook his head. "It'll be up to the police to sort this out."

Emily looked at Paul. "You must have been angry at Toby for losing your money like he did."

"I was. And I don't appreciate your tone. What are you implying? That I had something to do with his death?"

"No, of course not. You weren't even in town when it happened, right?"

"That's correct. Let me walk you out." Henry and Emily followed him to the door.

Paul said, "This has been stressful enough for both Lisa and Shari. Can you leave us alone now?"

"Of course. We'll let the police know she admitted Charlie and Toby were involved in the scheme and it's in their hands after that. Have a nice day." Emily followed Henry to the Jeep.

"Something still bugs me. Why did Paul lie about being in town at the time the murder took place?" said Emily.

"Maybe he wanted to lean on Toby about getting his money back and didn't want to upset Shari. At least one mystery is solved. And Charlie's off the suspect list."

"Something doesn't feel right with Paul. How about we stop at Coralee's and see if she remembers anything else about the night Paul stayed over?"

"I only had a cup of coffee this morning. I could go for Sunday brunch."

"Not that we need an excuse to talk to Coralee, but I can always be talked into brunch at the inn."

They pulled into the crowded parking lot. Coralee was standing in the lobby, handing out freshly baked blueberry mini muffins.

"Henry, Emily, good morning. Your parents haven't come down yet."

"We didn't have plans; this is a spontaneous stop. We just came from Lisa Cutler's place. She admitted Charlie and Toby were scheming together to sue the city and split the money."

"Seriously? Sounds like a movie plot."

"TV plot, actually. We called Megan on the way over. Toby was in serious financial trouble. He'd made a bad investment and lost not only most of his savings, but his son-in-law's as well."

"Well, I'll be darned. Guess that explains something Noah told me."

"Your son, Noah? Isn't he away at graduate school?"

"He was home a few weekends ago, helping me out while both Summer Martin and our new handyman were out of town. It was the same weekend Paul Townshend, Lisa's son-in-law, spent the night."

"What did he hear?"

"I didn't want to be a gossip, so I kept quiet. The day of the arts fair, Toby came here early Saturday to have lunch with Paul. It was busy, since half my guests were planning on going to the arts fair afterwards. I made them sandwiches, and when Noah brought the food to the table, he said Paul and Toby were arguing something fierce. He thought they were fighting about money."

Emily said, "You never told the police?"

"They didn't question me. Besides it was Noah who witnessed that incident."

"That incident? There's more?"

"Noah said Toby stormed out and Paul ran after him. Noah saw Toby leave, then Paul peeled out after him."

"That was the day of the fair. Coralee, maybe Paul followed him and killed him because of the argument. You have to call Megan."

"If you think it's important."

"I think it's very important. I heard Toby arguing with someone right before he took a dive off that roof. It could have been Paul."

"I'll call right now."

"Thanks, Coralee."

"Come and have some breakfast."

Henry said, "If we don't finish can I get a doggie bag?"

"You mean a container for the leftovers? Since when do you have leftovers, Henry? We have blueberry French Toast this morning."

"No, it's actually for a dog. Our dog, Spunky."

"You got yourself a dog! That's great. Emily mentioned getting herself a running companion but I didn't think she was serious being the devoted cat lover she is. What kind of dog is it?"

Emily said, "A terrier, pit bull, and assorted other breeds rolled into one. I don't think Spunky's going to be a great running companion, but Henry fell in love with him. He has three legs thanks to an ill-placed bear trap."

"Chester's okay with him?"

"So far, he pretty much ignores the dog. Doesn't like the barking—he runs away when Spunky barks," said Emily.

"Spunky only barks when he needs to go out," said Henry, sounding like a proud Papa.

"I can't wait to meet him. Come, the corner table is free. And we're all set for the bridal shower later this afternoon. Megan's coworker, Kim, dropped off the decorations yesterday and I've got the cake ready to go, it just needs to be frosted."

"I'd almost forgotten! I'll come by with Maddy and help decorate."

"After lunch service is over. Around 2:00?"

"Sounds good. I hope she doesn't know what we're planning."

"Kim said she's completely in the dark. Pat told her he's taking her to see a matinee at the playhouse in Woodbury."

"And she'll be fooled into thinking the inn is in Woodbury? Did Pat come up with this?"

"Henry, he'll make up an excuse about having to pick something up here first. Have faith in your friend."

"I'll take him for a beer while you're having the chick party."

Emily said, "Oh, no. This isn't your Mama's bridal shower. This is a couple's shower."

"Seriously?"

"You can chat outside with Pat and Drew while she opens the lingerie."

"Did you say lingerie?" Emily gave him a playful swat with the menu.

After brunch, they went home to find Maddy playing fetch with Spunky, Chester curled on the sofa next to her.

"Maddy, we brought you French Toast," said Emily. "And Coralee sent a handful of biscuits for Spunky."

She threw the toy, but instead of fetching, Spunky nuzzled up against Henry's leg. Henry reached down and scratched him behind the ears.

Maddy's phone buzzed. "I'll take this in my room."

They heard the door close behind her.

Henry said, "Since when does she talk on the phone? She always texts, right?"

"Yeah. Maybe she's talking to Jessica. It's encouraging that she still knows how to have a phone conversation."

"Something doesn't feel right." Spunky barked. "Okay, boy. Let's go for a walk."

Emily said, "No, I'll take him. It'll give us a chance to bond. Besides, I want to see if there's any possibility of him becoming a running buddy, though I think I already know the answer."

When Emily went out with Spunky, Henry tip-toed to Maddy's door and placed his ear against it.

"Yes, I'm keeping up my grades. We got a dog. He's got some pit bull in him so he'd hold his own there. No, he's only got three legs so not too much help as a bodyguard. Can I mail you cookies if I send it from my friend's address?"

Henry burst through the door. "Hang up."

"You can't make me."

"I said, hang up, now. Wait." He grabbed the phone. "If you ever call my daughter again I'll report it to the prison as harassment. Stay away from her." He slammed the phone on Maddy's bed.

"You have no right…"

"Are you insane? How did you get around the block?" He looked at the phone. "This isn't your phone!"

"My friend lent it to me. Her number isn't blocked. She's able to answer calls from the prison."

"Which friend? Wait until I talk to her parents."

"I'm not saying."

Henry grabbed the phone and said, "This belongs to Brooke."

"No, it doesn't."

"She has her initials on it in glitter! How stupid do you think I am?"

"I hate you. You can't stop me from talking to my own flesh and blood."

"You're grounded for a month."

"You can't do that. I'm helping with the games at Megan's shower this afternoon and the wedding is next week. Are you going to tell Megan I'm grounded and not allowed to be a bridesmaid?"

Henry grumbled. He'd have to discuss this with Emily. "Just wait and see." This time, it was him who slammed the bedroom door. He was fuming, ready to erupt like Mt. Etna. Just then, he heard Emily come back inside.

"This dog isn't going to be a running companion. Likes to stop and smell the roses every two feet and there aren't even roses to smell." She took off Spunky's leash. "Henry, what's wrong? You look furious."

"It's Maddy. She borrowed her friend Brooke's phone so she could take a call from the prison. You have to talk to Nancy about her, or better yet, I'll tell her how her daughter's an accomplice."

"Brooke lent Maddy her phone? Devious. Maddy's smart and she'll find any possible loophole when it comes to getting what she wants."

"I grounded her for a month."

"What about the shower and the wedding? It's not fair to Megan. Ground her with those two exceptions. I'll talk to her."

"Okay, but I'm so disappointed she can't see how this is wrong."

"She's not an adult, though I have to keep reminding myself as well. She's impulsive and thinks she knows it all. That's teenagers."

"But this is a safety issue. We have to put our feet down on this one."

"I totally agree. And Nancy will flip when she hears that Brooke lent Maddy the phone."

Maddy stayed in her room until it was time to leave for the shower. She gave Henry the silent treatment, and uttered one word responses to Emily's questions. Emily decided not to talk about the incident until after the shower. She'd gone alone to the inn to help set up while Maddy stewed in her room, then came back in time to change for the shower. Maddy came into the living room.

"Is that the dress we bought at the outlet mall? It looks so cute on you," said Emily.

"Cute? As in little girl cute? Just because you never had a little girl, don't try to make me into one."

It was a dumb comment meant to hurt and Emily, recognizing it as such, ignored it. "Let's get going or we'll be late.

Henry said "Goodbye, Spunky. Guard the house while we're gone." Then he went out started up the Jeep.

"Maddy, you got everything? Let's go or we'll be late."

"I hate Henry."

"You don't mean that, you're just angry. Your father and I want to keep you safe. It's our job."

"He's not my father."

She'd heard *you're not my mother* often enough to where it barely phased her. She'd never heard Maddy direct those words toward Henry.

Henry beeped the horn.

"We'll talk after the shower."

Chapter 17

The sun was out in full force and Emily hoped next weekend would be just as lovely for the wedding. She held a decorated box with a large bow on her lap.

Henry said, "What did we get them, anyway? Something leather that they'll both enjoy?"

"Hush. Maddy's right in the back."

"With those air pods stuck in her ears, she might as well be in Tel Aviv. She can't hear us."

"We, and by *we* I mean *I*, bought them a combination latte, cappuccino, espresso maker. A quick switch of the dial and it'll match any coffee house concoction."

"Seeing as there's only one Starbucks within a fifty-mile radius, it's a thoughtful gift."

He turned onto the drive leading to the inn.

"We have to park around back or Megan will recognize our car," said Emily.

"If this surprise gets by Megan, I'll have to question her detective abilities," said Henry. "Look at all those other cars in the lot? You think she won't recognize any as belonging to her friends?"

"Just come on before she shows up," said Emily. Maddy dragged her feet, lagging behind in her passive-aggressive protest to having parents hinder her life.

Coralee, in a cute yellow dress with matching comfort flats, shooed them inside. The room was decorated with pink and purple balloons, streamers, and centerpieces.

Maddy said, "This place looks like Barbie goes to the prom. Megan's a grown woman."

Henry said to Coralee, "Ignore her. She's in a snit."

Maddy glared at him then went across the room to her half-sister. Jessica turned around when she heard Maddy call her.

"Jessica, what happened to your eye?"

"Nothing, I walked into a wall."

"Jess, I'm not an idiot. Did Sam do this to you?"

"Shh. Okay, yes, but I don't want to ruin the shower. We can talk about it later. I thought I'd covered it up pretty well." She patted the area under her eye.

Maddy took powder foundation out of her purse and dabbed it gently on Jessica's bruise. "There. That's better. He isn't here, is he?"

"No, I didn't even tell him where I was going, but I wouldn't put it past him to have followed me."

"What's going on? Has he done this before?"

"He's never hit me before, but he's become verbally abusive in the past few weeks. Every time I try to break up with him he apologizes and gives me the same old sob story. His daughter died, and the grief has changed him."

"When did she die?"

"I think last year. He won't talk about it."

"He's been here for months and didn't act like that, did he? Or else you never told us."

"No, of course not. I never would have started dating him if he did. He used to be more easy-going. I guess that's how I'd describe it. Something changed him. Brought out this awful dark side. I think he needs to see a shrink and get on medication."

"This is it, though, right? You're breaking up with him?"

"Yes, of course. Coralee's herding everyone behind the tables. Come on."

The guests squeezed behind the tables while Coralee turned off the lights. When the door opened, they shouted surprise and judging by Megan's expression, it truly was a surprise. She threw her hands over her mouth and turned to Pat.

"You knew about this?"

"Yes. Kept a good secret, didn't I?"

"I'm impressed. Coralee, everyone, thank you. It's beautiful in here."

Coralee said, "We're all so happy for you and for Pat. It's about time Pat got another chance at happiness. After his wife died..."

Pat interrupted. "We aren't going to dwell on the past. A week from now we'll be Mr. and Mrs." He kissed Megan.

"Champagne for everyone," said Coralee. She looked at Maddy. "For all those legally of age. Otherwise, I have a stash of vintage sparkling apple cider."

The champagne matched the color of Megan's dress. When it was time to eat, Jessica headed to the table where Henry and Emily were seated.

"I don't want to sit with them," said Maddy.

"What? Don't be ridiculous. What happened?" said Jessica.

"I borrowed Brooke's phone so I could call our father in prison. Henry blocked my phone."

You did what? Why are you pursuing this, Maddy? You know how Henry, Emily, and I feel about you having contact with him. It's dangerous. He's a manipulative egotist. You have such a great father in Henry. You should be thanking the Lord every day."

"Says the woman who just let her boyfriend give her a black eye. You're a great judge of character." Maddy huffed and followed Jessica to the table. Drew and Frances came in and took seats at the same table.

Emily was surprised to see them. "Mom, I didn't think you knew Megan well enough to come to her bridal shower."

"I don't, but Coralee invited us. She knew you'd appreciate spending time with us before we leave."

Emily perked up. "You're leaving? When?"

"The end of the week. Hopefully we'll have a lead on Amy by then. Did you remember anything else since the hypnosis?"

"I think the kidnapper had a parrot on his shoulder."

"A parrot? Wouldn't you have heard a parrot, or were you that engrossed with your friends?"

"No, Mom. Parrots don't constantly chatter. That could be what attracted Amy to him. You know how she loved animals."

Frances corrected her. "Loves animals."

Henry said, "Pass the rolls." He noticed the buffet line. "I'm hungry. Anyone else going to join me?" He took the lead, piling his plate with miniature ham and turkey sandwiches, potato salad, deviled eggs, and green salad.

After the meal, Megan and Pat opened their presents, starting with the fancy coffee machine.

"Emily and Henry," said Megan. "We've been wanting one of these for a long time."

Pat said, "I'll bring an extra latte to the hospital for you." He skimmed the back of the box. "When I figure out how to use it."

"Give me the bow," said Emily. She started a paper plate bow-bouquet for the bride-to-be.

They opened Coralee's gift next.

"A cook book! Are these all recipes you cook here at the inn? This will make Pat very happy."

"Seeing as I do most of the cooking, yeah. Thank you, Coralee." Pat stacked the book on top of the coffee machine.

"My pleasure."

Megan and Pat sat with the Fox family for cake.

Emily wasn't planning on discussing business but couldn't resist. "Megan, have you checked out Paul Townshend, Lisa Cutler's son-in-law? Coralee says she heard him arguing with Toby the day of the arts fair and he followed him out."

Henry said, "Don't make her talk business at her wedding shower."

"I don't mind," said Megan. "Go on."

"Toby must have arrived at the arts fair a short time later. We arrived a little after noon and passed Toby near the entrance. Toby made a bad investment which affected Paul. He wanted his money back."

"I know. I checked into him. I know he was here at the inn the night before the murder, although Lisa and the daughter thought he'd arrived later."

"I heard someone cussing at Toby just before he went up to the roof. I'm not positive about the voice, but I think it could have been Paul."

"That's a good theory, however, Paul wasn't at the fair that day. He may have tried to follow Toby, but he had car trouble along Orchard Road. I have the invoice from the towing company. Paul has an alibi. He was dealing with his car when the murder took place."

She should have known Megan wouldn't have left that stone unturned. "Then why did he hide the fact he was in town the day before the murder?"

"He told us he was hoping to get his money back and surprise his wife before the baby comes. That's why he was here with Toby the day of the murder."

"Do you know about Toby's scheme to recoup the money?"

"You mean the fake lawsuit? Yes. As a matter of fact, Charlie Adams came into the station this morning to confess. I guess his conscience got the better of him."

"Will he go to jail?"

"He didn't actually go through with it and steal the money from the city, so no jail time, but he'll have some sort of consequence."

"Like a fine?"

"Or community service."

"No more shop talk. Let's enjoy this lovely shower."

"It's okay. I'd love to have this case wrapped up before the wedding next weekend and I have a million things on my schedule before then. I appreciate the legwork, as long as you don't put yourself in danger or interfere with the case."

Henry said, "Are you ready to go? Spunky's probably missing us and may need a walk."

"Megan, you and Pat will have to drop by and see our new family member."

"Maddy told me about him. That's wonderful."

Maddy came by. "Can we go now?"

"We'll say our goodbyes and be on our way." Henry grabbed his coat off the back of his chair. "Pat, I'll see you at the hospital tomorrow."

"Remember we have to pick up the tuxes after work."

"Got it."

Chapter 18

The next morning, Emily went for a run. Without Spunky. He was still curled up next to Henry, who'd carried him up the ladder to the loft the night before. When she got back, she was surprised Maddy wasn't yet awake.

She knocked on her door. "Maddy, you're going to be late for school. Are you awake? Maddy, open the door." She knocked so hard there was no way Maddy could have slept through the sound. "Maddy, I'm coming in."

She looked at the bed, which hadn't been slept in. Maddy's backpack, which usually sat on her desk, was gone, as was her phone. She ran to Henry, who by this time had just gotten out of the shower.

"Henry, Maddy's gone!"

"What do you mean gone? Maybe she had to be at school early for math club or something."

"No, the bed hasn't been slept in. Maddy never makes her bed—I did it for her yesterday."

"Call her friends. Call Jessica."

She couldn't hold the phone steady. Maddy was angry. What if she ran away? "Brooke, it's Emily. Have you heard from Maddy? Is she at school with you?"

"No. I haven't talked to her since I got my phone back from her yesterday."

"Were there any practices or club meetings at school this morning that she didn't tell us about?"

"No. Why?"

"If you see or hear from her, call us immediately, okay?"

"Yeah. Is everything okay?"

"I certainly hope so." She had a terrible feeling in her stomach.

Henry said, "I called Jessica. She hasn't heard from her. What about your parents? Maybe she stayed at the inn with them last night because she wanted to give us a scare."

"No way. We need to call the police."

"I don't think they'll do anything until she's been gone 24 hours."

"Megan took the day off to finish wedding errands. Her mother's coming in this afternoon. If we call the police, they'll take forever asking questions before they even consider looking for her. I have an idea. Come on."

Emily led Henry to Rebecca and Abby's cabin. "Rebecca's a computer whiz. She'll know how to find her. Maddy had to have money if she ran away." She checked her purse. "My credit card is missing."

Rebecca opened the door. "What's wrong? You two look like you've seen a ghost or something."

"It's Maddy. She ran away last night."

"That doesn't sound like her."

Henry said, "I have a feeling she'll try to go to Chicago to see her father."

"Isn't her father in jail?"

"Yes. And he's only a sperm donor. I'm her father."

Rebecca opened her computer. "First, we'll check flights to Chicago."

"I think the credit card company would have alerted me if she'd made a big purchase."

"What about a bus?" said Henry. "Check the buses. She left last night."

Emily checked her account. "Yes, there was a purchase made to Greyhound yesterday."

Rebecca clicked the keys. "There was a Greyhound bound for Chicago that left last night."

"Can you get into the passenger list?"

"Give me a minute." She worked her magic. "Bingo. She was on this bus." She showed the screen to Emily. "It's a sixteen-hour bus ride. If she left at 10 p.m., she'd be arriving around noon."

Henry said, "We can catch a flight and get there around the same time."

Rebecca said, "I'm ahead of you. Here's the flight schedule. Feel free to use the computer."

"Thanks. There's a flight leaving in an hour from Burlington. Think we can make it?"

"You'd better fly," said Rebecca.

Emily hugged her. "Thank you."

"Good luck. Maddy's smart and she lived in Chicago, right? She'll be okay."

Henry jumped in the Jeep and they took off to the airport, breaking every speed limit along the way.

"I can't believe she did this," said Emily. "I thought she had more sense. A young girl riding a bus alone at night? What if…"

"It's a reputable bus company. At least she didn't try to hitch hike. I'm going to ground her for a year when we find her."

Emily looked at her watch. "I don't think we'll make it in time to board."

Henry stepped on the gas. "Yes, we will." He sped through the entrance to the airport. "There's valet parking. Come on, let's get out of here."

He threw the keys to the valet. They ran to the long security line. Henry said, "Excuse me but our flight leaves in ten minutes. Can we please cut ahead? Our daughter—she ran away and we have to get to her."

The crowd was sympathetic. They allowed them to cut to the front of the line. Emily breezed through, but Henry set off the alarm.

"Henry, come on! We're going to miss the plane!"

He took his keys out of his pocket and tried again. The alarm sounded, provoking irritated looks from those in line behind him who were most likely regretting letting him cut ahead at this point.

"Sir, we'll have to have you step aside." The TSA worker held a wand. Henry couldn't stop his foot from tapping and tried to quiet his sighs.

At last he was good to go. He held his shoes under his arm. He grabbed Emily's hand and they ran through the airport like OJ Simpson in the old luggage commercials.

"This is our gate," said Emily. "Oh no! Don't close the door!"

Henry, out of breath, begged. "Please, don't close it." He shoved the boarding pass in front of the woman's face. "Our daughter ran away. She's fourteen, all alone in Chicago."

Emily said, "Do you have children?"

The door opened and a flight attendant said, "I heard shouting. Is something wrong?"

"Emily fumbled with her words. "We need to get on this plane. Our daughter...she's trying to visit her father. Her real, I mean biological, I mean sperm donor..."

Henry said, "Please. It'll take an extra three minutes to let us on."

"Okay. Go ahead." She stepped aside. "I hope your daughter is okay."

"Thank you." Henry grabbed Emily's hand and led her onto the plane. When they got to their row, Emily slumped into the seat and caught her breath.

"We'll be there in under two hours," said Henry. "We'll take a cab to the prison. It'll cost a fortune, but I don't want to waste any time renting a car."

Emily couldn't focus enough to read on her phone. She tried closing her eyes, but all she saw was Maddy being grabbed…Maddy crying…Maddy in a prison waiting room. After what seemed like a glacially slow fight, they finally made it off the plane and into a cab.

"Greenville Prison. Hurry," said Henry.

The cab driver snaked through the airport but was hit with Chicago traffic.

"Can you step on it?"

"Henry, what's he supposed to do? He can't fly over the cars. If she's at the prison, ironically, she'll be somewhere safe." She said those words, but inside wanted to strangle the driver until he bumped through all the other cars.

"There's a sign for the prison," said Henry. He grabbed his wallet from his pocket. "Let us out in front." He threw a wad of twenties at the driver.

"Do you think she's here yet?" said Emily. She looked up at the barbed wire fence, the guard house, and the stark concrete exterior of the prison. She shuddered.

"Depends on whether or not the bus was on time." They ran toward the entrance. "Hey, isn't that her? Sitting on the stoop?"

"I think so. Come on, let's go." Emily got to her first.

"Maddy, we were so worried. Are you okay?" Emily hugged her sobbing daughter.

"I came all this way and they won't let me see my father. I'm not old enough. I have to see him. I have to know what he's like. It's my father."

Emily sympathized, but was at a loss for words. She was glad the prison hadn't let her in by herself.

Henry said, "Then let's go in."

Emily did a double take. "Did you say we're going in?"

"If she wants to meet her father, we'll all meet her father."

"Really?" said Maddy. She stopped sniffling. "I thought you were against this."

"I am, but I know how stubborn you are. Maybe if you see once and for all what he's like, you'll be satisfied and not try something like this again. Come on." He led the march toward the prison entrance.

They went through security and waited for visiting hours to begin. Emily shivered. This wasn't a place she wanted to be. Henry had shocked her with this suggestion.

The guard came out. "Visiting hours have begun." Maddy followed her parents to the visitor's room. Emily was expecting to be seated behind glass, but instead they were led to a cold, gray room with metal tables and plastic chairs. The guard pointed to a balding man with a paunch wearing an orange jumpsuit. "That's him." They sat down across the table from him. Emily hadn't expected this. *No one would guess he'd been a prominent doctor in another lifetime.*

"So who are you? My daughter? Is this the Maddy I spoke to on the phone? The one who answered my letters?"

Emily's skin crawled as she caught a whiff of his stinky breath. "And we're her parents. She wants to see you in the flesh, but this is the end of it."

He sat back in the chair, crossing his arms over his chest, looking Maddy up and down. "So this pretty lady is Maddy. You have my eyes."

Maddy cringed. So did Emily. Henry resisted the urge to slug him.

"What do you want to know about me?"

"Why did you lie to my mother?" Maddy never sounded more like a little girl.

"Lie? She wanted a baby and I gave her a baby. I'd call it win-win. You've got half your genes from a Mensa member."

"How many children have you fathered? I have half brothers and sisters running around that I'll never know."

"Populate the world with cream of the crop genes. You're lucky, Maddy. Those sperm donors do it for the money. And no matter what they tell you, we have no way of knowing if they are drug addicts, secretly harbor mental illness, or have some hidden physical flaw. I did those women a favor. And you're a pretty young lady. I didn't do too badly." He blew her a kiss. Henry started to lean over the table. Emily pulled him back.

"I'll bet you're smart, too. Look at those broad hips. You'll make it through natural selection and carry on my legacy."

Emily could see by Maddy's expression she was mortified. Emily stood and leaned across the table. "Don't you dare."

Now Henry touched his wife's shoulder and said, "Come on, Maddy. Have you seen enough?"

"Maddy's going to stay in touch. Someday I'll be outta here and we'll do Sunday dinners." He laughed an eerie laugh.

"Let's go," said Emily. Maddy stood up.

"How about a little sugar before you leave, daughter of mine?" The beast puckered his lips.

Henry walked around the table and looked the doctor squarely in the eyes. "Leave my daughter alone. I hope you rot in here and rot in hell afterwards." Henry saw the fear in Maddy's ashen face and grabbed his daughter by the arm in a protective reflex. "Let's go." She followed willingly.

The guard opened the door with a hand-held remote. Henry had a momentary flash. *The door is radio controlled. It sends a signal and the guard doesn't even have to touch the handle. Of course!*

Chapter 19

Emily booked a red-eye back to Sugarbury Falls, while Henry called Kurt and asked him to feed and walk Spunky. When they arrived back home and fell into bed, it was nearly dawn.

After a few hours of sleep, Henry headed out to the hospital while Emily and Maddy slept in. Given the circumstances, and confident she'd have no trouble making up the work, they'd decided to let Maddy miss another day of school.

Pat pulled into the hospital parking lot at the same time as Henry.

"Hey, you stood me up. We were supposed to meet at the formal wear store after work yesterday. Your tux is ready."

"I'm sorry. You have no idea what we went through yesterday. Maddy ran away to go visit her sperm donor dad in prison."

"Is she okay? Isn't he in jail in Chicago?"

"Yep. She's home safe and sound. She took a bus out there and we hopped on the first flight we could find to chase after her."

"Good thing you stopped her."

"We didn't. Not really. I decided it was time to get this out of her head once and for all, so the three of us met with him."

"You're kidding, right?"

"No. And he's a fat, stinky, jackass. I'm glad Maddy saw him for what he is."

"It must be so hard raising kids. I know Megan wants children. I'm not sure I can handle it, especially at my age."

"You can do it. If I was able to step up and parent a teen-ager, you'll be able to manage someone who doesn't run away and sass you back. Seeing that monster in an orange jumpsuit, I felt so protective of Maddy. It's like some sort of instinct. If he or anyone else tried to hurt her, I'd go off the deep end. I'd kill to protect her."

"Well, I guess I'd be getting used to it gradually. Can you pick up your tux tonight?"

"Will do. I'll be expecting that latte you promised me."

"Megan already has your generous, albeit complicated, gift out on the counter."

"I want to bounce an idea off you. Toby Cutler had that ICD implanted. What if someone set it off so he'd have a heart attack up on that roof?"

"Well, why do that? Why not push him off, or induce a heart attack on the ground?"

"Suppose the murderer was physically unable to push Toby off the roof? Toby was a big guy."

"You have to be within a certain proximity range to set those things off, don't you?"

"Yes. If the killer wasn't someone Toby would have had over to his house for dinner, then he would have needed to find a different way to get close."

"So corner him at a public event, right? He could blend right in. Then again, with a crowd around, someone might know CPR and there'd be a chance for a rescue."

"But not if he fell off the roof. And it'd seem like natural causes, not necessarily a murder," said Henry. "Why didn't his doctor have any information about the implant surgery? Toby's daughter knew the hospital where he had it done, but when I called, they had no record of a Toby Cutler. It's too bad the serial number wasn't readable."

"Did you check with Megan? I gave her the device to take to the crime lab to see if they could decipher the number."

"That's right, I'd forgotten you did that. I'll give her a call this morning."

Henry had a few patients waiting in the ER to be seen. When he finished, he called Megan.

"Henry, let me check. Yes, I got the report back. They were able to make out the serial number, want it?"

"Yes, please."

She read off the number. "We know who the victim is. How's this going to help?"

"I have a hunch. I'll get back to you."

After he hung up, he ran the number through the data base. *How is this possible? It's registered to someone else. To someone named Troy Cambridge.*

A nurse poked her head in. "You have a patient. She asked for you specifically."

Henry closed his computer and was surprised to see Jessica waiting in the cubical.

"What's wrong, Jessica?"

"It's my arm. I think it's broken."

"What happened? Trying to climb a tree at recess?"

"Not funny. Sam did this to me when I told him I wanted to break up. I'd never seen him be this violent. If he comes back, I'm getting a restraining order."

"I'm so sorry. I never liked the guy but I didn't know he was dangerous."

"I'll kick him to the curb, but the problem is I have to work at the same school and we'll inevitably run into each other."

Concerned for both her mental and physical state, he prioritized. "First, let's take a look at your arm. Then we'll talk about calling the police."

She held it out. "It hurts a lot and it's swelling up."

"I'll get an x-ray and with luck you won't need surgery."

"Surgery?"

"Only if it's a complicated fracture. Otherwise you'll just need a cast. I'll order the x-rays." He pointed to her eye. "What happened there?"

"Nothing, really." She looked away while answering. "Will I be okay to go to school tomorrow?"

He knew Sam had to be responsible for the black eye as well as the arm. "Even if you don't need surgery, you'll need a cast, and it's bound to be sore. You should take off tomorrow. And on second thought, let's call the police right now."

"No, I'll stay clear of him and it'll be okay. I'm kind of embarrassed over the situation."

"Why? It's not your fault."

"I was stupid enough not to see this side of him and not to have the strength to break up when I sensed things weren't right. Even after he gave me this black eye."

"Think about it. We'll talk later."

He felt a bit fatherly toward Jessica given she was Maddy's sister and they shared that poor excuse for a biological father. He'd talk to her again after the arm was set and she'd gotten some rest.

He checked on a woman who thought she'd had a heart attack, but fortunately the chest pain had been brought on by a bad case of indigestion. Then, he went back to his office to pick up where he'd left off. He called his *Words with Friends* buddy, the doctor down in Florida who he thought may have inserted Toby's

ICD. He was fortunate to reach him in the middle of a work day.

"You again? Calling to gloat over that 130 point-word you played? Guess when you get to be retired you have time to come up with those moves."

"Which 130-point word? The one I played last night or the one I played this morning?"

"I'm going to hang up now."

"Just kidding. The one this morning was only 90 points, but I'm not calling to gloat."

"You could've fooled me."

"I need a favor. Last time we spoke, I asked about a patient named Toby Cutler. You said he'd never been your patient. I have the serial number of the ICD and ran it through the data base. Turns out the man has been using a different name. Did you insert the ICD into a man named Troy Cambridge?"

"Give me a few minutes. This patient would have shown ID and an insurance card, no doubt. Why do you think he was using a false name?"

"I think his name is Troy Cambridge, and Toby Cutler is the false name. I don't know what he was hiding, but chances are it's what got him killed."

"I found him. What do you want to know?"

"Are you able to access his data? It was a newer model. Correct?"

"The data was collected. I'd have to go through it. Might take time."

"Would you look at the date and time I'm about to text you and see if you observe anything strange? Did he have a heart attack or any other cardiac event?"

"I have a full schedule. It may take a while, but I'll get back to you."

"It could be the key to solving a murder case. Thanks. Good luck at the medical conference. I see you're one of the keynote speakers. Congrats."

"Thanks. We'll talk soon."

After he hung up, he called Emily. "Hey, hon. Is Maddy up yet?"

"No, she's fast asleep. Your dog has been looking for you. He keeps looking up the ladder to the loft and whining."

"Put him on the phone."

"You can't be serious."

"You don't think it'd help if he hears my voice?"

"Look, I've got to get over to the college."

"Okay, listen. Toby Cutler was using a false name. His real name is Troy Cambridge. I spoke to the doctor in Florida who implanted the ICD and he's going to go through the data and see if Toby, I mean Troy, had a heart attack up on that roof."

"A false name? Why? And Lisa was going by Cutler, too. Do you think she's also using a fake name?"

"I don't know. He was hiding something, obviously, and most likely if we find out what it was, we'll find the killer. Can you talk to Lisa?"

"I guess I can stop by on the way to work. What if she denies it? Or doesn't know he was using an alias?"

"Just start from there, okay?"

"Sure."

"One more thing. Jessica is here in the ER."

"Jessica? What happened? Is she hurt?"

"That boyfriend of hers gave her a broken arm. You have to talk to her. She says she's going to break up with him but I have a feeling it won't be easy. I tried to convince her to call the police."

"Maddy disliked him from the start. I have a class this afternoon but I'll drop by her place on the way."

"I'm being paged. Got to go. Love you."

Chapter 20

Emily checked on Maddy, then headed over to Lisa Cutler's. She rang the bell, glad to see the car in her driveway.

Lisa wore jeans and a long-sleeved red t-shirt. Her hair was neatly brushed into a ponytail. "Emily? What can I do for you?"

"I wanted to check and see how you're doing. Did Shari and Paul go back home?"

"Yes. Shari has a doctor's appointment later today and they have a slew of things to do before the baby comes. Do you have news about Toby's murder?"

"Indirectly. The police lab was able to make out the serial number on Toby's ICD. It was registered to someone named Troy Cambridge. Doesn't make sense." She watched Lisa closely for a reaction. Lisa looked downward and shook her head.

"That's impossible. They must have mixed up the devices."

"I don't think so. The hospital has no record of a Toby Cutler."

"It must be a mistake."

"Did your husband change his name? It's important to know."

Lisa stuttered. "No. of course not." Lisa's house phone rang. "That might be Shari. I have to take it."

"Go on. I'll wait."

While she went to the kitchen to answer, Emily remembered exactly where the yearbook was on the shelf. She leafed through it looking for the name Troy

Cambridge. She heard Lisa coming back and quickly slammed it closed.

"I need my appointment book. I think I left it here somewhere." Lisa rifled through the stack of papers on the desk. "Got it. I'll be right back." She returned to the kitchen.

When she was sure Lisa was back in the kitchen and heard her talking on the phone, Emily opened the yearbook once again. She found the team sports page she was looking for. Right next to Charlie Adams's name, was a picture of Troy Cambridge. She examined it closely. *He looks like the boy in the team picture. That's the proof I need. Toby Cutler is actually Troy Cambridge. Why did he change his name? Did he swap identities with an old friend? Why Toby Cutler?*

She flipped to the senior portraits pages, which were arranged alphabetically. When she got to the C's, she leafed through. *Troy Cambridge, but no Toby Cutler. Lisa Cutler is listed right here. She looks the same as she does now. She'd mentioned they were high school sweethearts. So he took his wife's last name, but why?*

She stuck the yearbook back just as Lisa returned from the kitchen.

"I hope everything is okay. Was that your daughter?"

"Yes. She's fine. The doctor planned a C-section and she wants me to be there to help her when she gets out of the hospital. I was just checking my schedule."

"Lisa, would Shari know if Toby changed his name?"

"He didn't do that. I already told you."

She sensed Lisa was getting annoyed, but pushed onward. "When you married Toby, did you change your last name, or keep your maiden name? I'm asking for a friend. My friend is getting married this weekend and she's debating whether or not to take her husband's name. I've been asking all the married women I run into. I changed mine when I married Henry."

Lisa looked confused, then took a breath. "I was the last Cutler in my family. Our family came over on the Mayflower. My parents didn't have a son, and my grandfather's dying wish was that I continue the family name. So no, I didn't change my name."

"I read how some men actually take their wife's name! I get hyphenating, but giving up your own name is strange for a man, right?"

"Live and let live is my motto. Now, if you'll excuse me, I need to do some errands."

"Sure. I have a class to teach anyhow. I'll see myself out."

Emily called Henry on the way to the college. "Lisa denies knowing anything about a false name."

"Maybe he changed it before he met her. The ICD was implanted last year. If she didn't know, he'd have had to hide it when he went to the doctor and was admitted to the hospital. Is that possible?"

"I don't think so. Lisa's maiden name was Cutler. She didn't change it when they got married. Toby was hiding something—in addition to his friendship with Charlie Adams and the false lawsuit scheme."

"What reasons do people have for hiding? Owing money, breaking the law, being threatened by someone..."

"He admitted to being broke, but hadn't yet broken the law."

"As far as we know." His phone buzzed, indicating an incoming call. "I've got to go. We'll talk later."

Emily pulled in behind her building at St. Edwards. Since the arts fair, she viewed the campus differently. It had once been an insulated, safe college campus nestled in the mountains. Now, she had flashbacks to Toby's murder every time she looked around. The roof of the nearby building wasn't a just a place to get a bird's eye view of the campus. It was the last place Toby took a breath. The trail around the campus wasn't a scenic hiking path, but a muddy escape route for a killer. She hoped that feeling would fade over time.

She unlocked her office. Nancy happened to be passing by.

"Hey, Emily, how's Maddy? Brooke told me what happened."

"Quite a whirlwind. We were scared to death when she ran away. We caught up to her sitting outside the prison in Chicago. They wouldn't let her see her father given she was a minor."

"Thank God for that."

"Then, Henry surprised us both, saying we should all go in. I'd have dragged her away faster than anything."

"So you saw him?"

"Yep. Big, balding—looked like a giant pumpkin in his prison clothes. He was awful. Full of himself—made gross comments to Maddy."

"I'll bet Henry wanted to slug him."

"So did I! Anyway, Maddy saw him for what he was and now it's out of her system."

"I'm glad she's home today. Brooke texted me from school. They had a lock-down drill. Look what she sent me. *Had to practice hiding in a corner in the dark in case a shooter comes on school grounds.* At first they didn't tell them it was a drill and she had chest pains, she was so scared. What's this world coming to?"

"Of all places, you'd think Sugarbury Falls would be immune to such horrors. Then again, we had a murder right on our campus."

"And it wasn't the first!"

"You know, I'd about erased the other incident from my mind and it wasn't all that long ago."

"Hey, any news about your sister?"

"Not since the kidnapped victim escaped. Police found the burnt cabin and he's on the run, with Amy, I hope."

"You hope?"

"I'm sure she's slowing him down. What if he decides to leave her in the woods while he escapes, or worse?"

"He's been taking care of Amy for thirty years. I'll bet he truly cares about her and will keep her safe. It's only a matter of time before someone spots them."

"I hope you're right. I can only imagine how wonderful it would be to hug my sister again. If we had a bigger place, I'd have her move in with us. In fact, if we find her—I mean when we find her—maybe we'll add on to our cabin."

"I can't wait to meet your sister. I'll bet it will happen soon. I have a good feeling."

"Thanks, Nancy." On the way to class, she heard birds—the first she remembered hearing since the cold weather had set in. *Birds, man with a parrot, did I tell Megan?*

After she finished teaching, she called Megan. "How's the bride to be holding up? Nervous?"

"I'm more excited than nervous. Mom is in town and I'm taking off the rest of the week to prepare last minute details. Pat won't tell me where we're going for our honeymoon but he said to pack a bathing suit and warm weather clothes. Thought Mom and I would head to the outlet mall."

"The Cruise Cabinet has nice swimsuits at good prices. It's right next to the food court. I hate to bother you on your time off."

"Go on, what's on your mind?"

"I remembered under hypnosis that Amy's kidnapper had a bird. A parrot, I think. Can you make sure the police in Watuga know that? They'll take you more seriously than if I call. I mean, it's been thirty years so I could be grasping at straws, but parrots live a long time, right?"

"So I've heard. I'll make the call. It can't hurt."

"Thanks, Megan."

"By the way, I booked my hair stylist for the morning of the wedding and I told her to leave time to do you and Maddy if you'd like."

"That's so nice of you." She'd completely forgotten to make an appointment at her regular salon. "Maddy will be excited, she's been looking at up dos on Pinterest. Not sure how much she can do with mine, it barely stretches into a ponytail."

"You'd be surprised. Anyway, it'll be fun. My Mom says she'll make mimosas and pick up something from the bakery."

"I can't wait. We've known Pat since we moved here and it's wonderful to see how happy you've made him. He went through so much when Carol died."

"Well, he's turned my life around as well. I'll talk to you during the week."

"Have fun with your mom."

Chapter 21

Henry exchanged his white coat for a jacket. He was about to stick his phone in his pocket when it vibrated. It was Toby's doctor from Florida.

"Henry, I've got news for you. I was able to access the data on Troy Cambridge. I looked at the date you mentioned and found something strange."

"Strange? Like he had a heart attack?"

"Like there was a surge—a shock to his heart."

"Maybe it was going out of rhythm so it shocked him. Isn't that what those machines do?"

"This was more than that. And he wasn't having any sort of cardiac event immediately before it happened."

"Was it a malfunction?"

"More like interference. Like the stimulation came from an outside source."

"Is that even possible?"

"Theoretically. If someone knew what they were doing, they could cause such a surge remotely."

"Great. Then the perpetrator could be in another state."

"No. There's a limited range. To do this from outside, it had to be within a certain number of feet."

He remembered Pat saying that as well. "Wouldn't you have gotten some sort of an alert?"

"Under normal circumstances, of course. Unless there was external electromagnetic interference. I can't imagine with all the safeguards built into the device, but if someone knew enough about the field and deliberately tried to interfere with the signal, it could happen. When remote monitoring came into use, the risk was highly debated, however, the benefits outweighed the remote chance of that happening."

"Remote chance? Interesting choice of words. So if someone wanted to murder a person with such a device, he could be within a certain number of feet and cause a shock which wouldn't set off an alarm?"

"It's a bit science fiction, and I've never heard of an actual case, but I think it's possible."

"If a person then had a cardiac event, could he be resuscitated by CPR?"

"Yes, if there were people around to notice—just like with a naturally occurring cardiac event."

"So you'd have to isolate the person to insure it would work as a murder method?"

"Henry, is there something you're hiding?"

"No, it's hypothetical."

"And for a friend, right?"

"Troy Cambridge was going by an assumed name. He moved to our town last year and at a recent arts fair, he fell or was pushed off a roof. Witnesses say they heard arguing and saw another person fleeing the scene. What I don't get though, is why not just push him off the roof? Why go through all that technical mumbo jumbo?"

"Was he a big guy? Hmmm, looking at these medical records, he weighed in at 250 pounds at the time of his visit. Ever try to push someone that size?"

"But if he was incapacitated..."

"Brilliant. Weaken him, then push him off the roof, leaving people to think he fell off."

"Can you forward his records to the Sugarbury Falls Police for me?"

"Will do. By the way, I'm sitting on a J, Q, and Z. And I see the triple word spaces are still available."

"Thanks. For forwarding the records, I mean. Keep in touch."

After finishing the call, he checked to see if Jessica's x-rays were ready to view. Trained as a radiologist, he was relieved to see immediately that the break wouldn't require surgery. He went to tell Jessica the news before heading home.

"Henry, did you get the x-rays back? Will I need surgery?"

"Luck was on your side. No surgery, just a cast. We have a super orthopedic guy on staff. I'll set you up with him."

"Thanks, Henry. Can I go home now?"

"Are you sure you feel safe going back to your place? Let me take you down to the police station to file a report, first."

"I just want to go home. If Sam comes anywhere near my house, I'll kick his butt right back to Florida in a heartbeat. Besides, I'll have to see him at work and don't want to provoke him. Provided he doesn't get his lazy behind fired."

"I still say you should report this to the police."

"I'll be okay. Thanks, Henry."

When Henry got home, Spunky ran to him, tail wagging wildly.

Emily said, "That dog of yours whined at the window from the time I got home until you walked through the door."

Henry scratched Spunky between the ears, then scooped him up in his arms. Spunky licked his face.

"Henry, you shouldn't let him lick your face. You're a doctor. You know how many germs a dog has in his mouth, right?"

He spoke to the dog. "My Spunky's a good dog. Who has germs? Not you, right, boy."

Emily shook her head. "How's Jessica?"

"The arm is broken but she won't need surgery. I hope she's serious about kicking Sam to the curb. He's dangerous. Next time it might be more than a broken arm."

"Didn't she say it was over?"

"Yes, but you know how this could play out. He'll show up with a dozen roses and swear it'll never happen again and how sorry he is."

"Jessica's a strong lady."

"I know, but these wife beater types are very manipulative. You should have a talk with her. I hope Maddy never winds up in this sort of a situation. I'd kill anyone who laid a finger on her, I swear." He thought about how he wanted to strangle Maddy's prisoner father when he started making those suggestive comments to her. He put Spunky down on the floor and grabbed the leash. "I'll take the dog for a walk. What have you got for dinner?"

"A reservation at Coralee's. I told my mother we'd meet them for dinner."

"Okay. See you in a bit. Maddy's home, right?"

"She's in her room doing homework. She was having trouble with her laptop earlier but I think she resolved it."

"Oh, by the way, I spoke to Toby's, I mean Troy's, doctor down in Florida. I think someone lured Toby to the roof, then caused him to have a heart attack by interfering with his ICD."

"How'd you come up with that?"

"Hear me out. Toby's a big guy. It would have been difficult to push him off that roof."

"If someone was able to interfere with the signal, and by that I assume you mean cause a heart attack?"

"Exactly."

"Why the roof?" said Emily. "Why not at his house or in the midst of the arts fair?"

"There's a range of accessibility. Maybe he didn't know Toby well enough to show up at his house or meet him for lunch, so he had to do it in a public place."

"That's true."

"Think about it. If Toby had a heart attack in the middle of the fair, the chances of someone knowing CPR or calling 911 were great. I was there, for example. I would have tried to revive him and very possibly would have succeeded. No guarantee the heart attack would have done him in."

"So he isolated him, and incapacitated him…"

"Then it would have been easy enough to push him off the roof, guaranteeing his death."

"So it had to be someone who knows about electronics."

"Or programming, or how medical devices work."

"But what's the motive? What threat was an over-weight, sixty-year-old man to anyone?"

"You said yourself he lost a bundle in that bad investment. And his son-in-law was one of the ones who lost out."

"And he snuck into town the day before the murder. He works in the technology field! I heard him say he was tired of fixing computer glitches when Lisa mentioned her laptop wasn't responding."

"And you can find just about anything on YouTube these days. Maybe it wasn't as complicated to interfere with the device as we think."

"Wait a minute. Megan said he had an alibi. He had car trouble and was waiting for a tow truck when the murder happened."

"I should call Megan. Wait. She's with her mother doing wedding stuff."

"When does Ron Wooster get back from vacation?"

"Tomorrow, I think. I'll talk to him tomorrow. Maybe you should come with me since you spoke to his doctor down in Florida."

Spunky tugged at the leash. "Okay. We'll do that."

Emily sat on the sofa and from out of nowhere, Chester flew onto her lap. She grabbed the brush from under the coffee table and made Chester's black fur shine as he reveled in the attention. Then she called to check on Jessica. Soon Henry and Spunky were back.

"I'll change and we can head to the inn," said Henry. "Spunky's making friends. We ran into Kurt and Prancer. Prancer's twice his size, but it didn't stop our boy here from walking right up to him and sniffing his tail."

"Spoken like a proud Dad. I think he and Milo will be friends as well. We'll have to bring him by Rebecca and Abby's soon. I'll tell Maddy to get ready."

Chapter 22

Frances and Drew came into the lobby just as the Fox family arrived at Coralee's.

"Emily, I have some news," said Frances. "The Watuga police contacted me. Someone called into the tip line. They spotted a man and woman who fit the description of Amy and the kidnapper. They're going to keep searching the area. I feel like we're getting close."

"The description could fit many people. An older man and a forty-something woman?"

"With a parrot? The man had a parrot on his shoulder!"

"Mom, that's incredible. What if it's them?"

"I'm ready to drive to Watuga tomorrow. Want to come?"

Emily looked at Henry for approval. He nodded his head. "Okay. I'll have to cancel my classes tomorrow. How long are you planning on staying?"

"Until they find them."

"Megan's wedding is Saturday. I'll have to be back before then."

"I'm hoping by then we'll have Amy in our arms again."

Coralee, menus in hand, said, "I saved your favorite table by the window. Maddy, another cat and her two kittens were adopted this morning by one of my guests. They'll be making their home a few hours from here."

"Magpie, Marco, and Layla?"

"Yes. Isn't that great? You really made a difference with your community service project."

"Thanks."

Emily said, "Coralee, remember you said Paul, Toby Cutler's son-in-law, argued with Toby and left the inn close to when the arts fair started?"

"Yes, that's right. You thought he hadn't arrived in town yet."

"The police said he had car trouble and thus has an alibi for the time Toby fell off the roof. Did he have a rental car by any chance? You have a record of your guests' cars, right? When I went to Lisa Cutler's house, I only saw one car in the driveway but both Shari and Paul were at the house."

"I'll check as soon as I have a minute."

"Thanks."

Henry said, "Why does it make a difference if he had a rental?"

"The police said he called the local towing company. When you rent a car, don't they have their own roadside service?"

"Even so, the alibi was verified."

"Don't you think it's possible he bribed someone at the repair shop to give him an alibi?"

"It's a bit far-fetched, don't you think?"

"I guess. It's just, if you had a rental and it had a problem, why not just switch out the car? Especially if you were intending to fake arriving the next day."

"He would have had motive, means, and opportunity if he'd made it to the arts fair."

"And don't forget, technical knowledge."

Frances said, "Enough murder talk. What are you having for dinner?"

Henry browsed the specials. "Clam chowder for starters."

Maddy said, "She has squash casserole on the menu. I'm having that with a side of pasta."

Coralee returned. "Yes, he had a rental car. You were right."

After dinner, Frances and Drew sat out beyond the porch. Coralee had recently installed a fire pit which seemed to be very popular with the guests. Emily was exhausted, yet her mind was full thinking about arranging to leave town for a few days.

When they got home, Emily flicked on the lights and gasped. "Oh my God. What happened here?" The house looked as though it had been ransacked. Books were pulled off the shelf. Ripped paper was everywhere. One of the sofa pillows had its stuffing strewn all over the floor. Her first thought was robbery. "What if the robber is still in the house? Call the police, Henry." Then she spotted a wagging tail from under the sofa cushion. She took a breath.

"Spunky! Bad dog," said Emily. Spunky ran to Henry.

"What did you do, boy? "Henry picked up the books. "He must have missed me."

"Next time we're putting him in his crate when we leave the house. Unless you want to take him with us."

"Would Coralee let us take him to the inn and eat with us? I mean, she has a bunch of cats upstairs."

Emily said, "I meant that as a joke. We have to train Spunky not to destroy the house because we're gone. He didn't do this before."

"We never left him all alone after dark. We can try leaving the lights on next time."

"Sure. We'll put him in his crate and leave the living room light on. Maybe play some classical music for him too." Before Henry could tell her it was a great idea, she said, "Lights, yes. I was kidding about the music."

"I'll clean this up. Go take a bath and relax. You have a long car ride tomorrow."

"Okay. I have to pack a few things and want to turn in. We're planning an early start."

Emily threw a few items in a suitcase, then tried to fall asleep. It was impossible. She was too excited thinking about the possibility of seeing Amy again. She wished she had time to pick up some chocolates or a small gift. Would Amy remember her? It'd been a long time. In her heart, she felt the bond between sisters was strong enough to withstand the separation. If they found her, would her mother and Drew take her in, or was she able to live on her own after all these years? Could she and Henry have her live with them? The questions kept coming and it was hours before she shut her eyes for the night.

"Emily, your phone!" said Henry.

Emily opened her eyes. The sun was beginning to stream through the window. "What is it?"

"Your phone. Didn't you hear it buzzing?"

She groped for it. "Mom? I'll be ready in half an hour."

She heard sobs through the phone. "We're not going."

"Why not?"

"The Watuga police called a little while ago. The information they got was a cruel joke. Some teenagers thinking it would be funny to make a call to the tip line."

"Why on Earth would they do that? And how did they know about the parrot?"

"The information leaked out on social media. They were probably hoping for a reward."

Her head ached. "I'm so sorry. And so disappointed. We'll get another lead. They couldn't have gotten far. The police didn't find a record of a passport, and the train and bus stations have been alerted. They must be in the area somewhere."

"Drew hired a private detective."

"Great. Between him, the police, and us, we're bound to find her soon." She wished she believed her words.

"I have the PI checking the morgues and hospitals all over New England. So far nothing. What if they made it to Canada?"

"She'd need a passport. According to the Watuga police, she doesn't have one. Maybe this PI Drew hired will find a clue soon. I'll keep my bag packed in case he does and we need to get there in a hurry."

"Okay. Drew and I are going to go down for breakfast. I'll call you later."

"Sooner if you hear something."

Henry said, "I take it the trip is canceled."

"Postponed, for now. What a cruel joke, those boys calling the tip line like they did."

"I know. If you have the time today, maybe you can check on Jessica. She may need help getting groceries or doing errands with the cast on."

"I'll give her a call. Is Maddy up?"

"Yeah. She took Spunky for a walk."

"Did he…"

"Yes, he had a minor accident but I cleaned it up."

"I know how to spend my time today. I'm going to research getting this dog trained. Good thing you didn't bring him up here last night."

"Actually, be careful getting out of bed. The rug may still be a little wet."

She threw the pillow at him as he left the room.

After breakfast, she called Jessica.

"How's your arm?"

"It hurts. I'm trying to figure out how to negotiate a shower. Are you on the way to upstate New York?"

"No, unfortunately the tip turned out to be a hoax."

"I'm sorry."

"Yeah, I'm disappointed to say the least. Drew hired a private investigator. Maybe he'll turn up something. Meanwhile, let's talk about Sam."

"There's really nothing to talk about. I'm having the locks changed and I'll find a way to deal with him at school."

"I can take you to the police station to make a report."

"I don't want to. I'll be okay."

"Don't get caught alone with him."

"I won't."

"You said he was married before. Do you think he acted this way toward his ex-wife?"

"I don't know. They had a daughter who died. I think that's when things went south. Are you going into work now that your plans are canceled?"

"No, I've got my TA covering. I think I'll try to make some progress on my book and maybe research dog behavior. Hey, do you feel up to going out for lunch?"

"Sure. Want to meet downtown? We can browse a little, though most of the clothing in those shops is out of my budget."

"Sounds good. See you then."

Emily tried to concentrate on writing her latest true crime book but her mind kept wandering. Spunky sat at the window, pining for Henry. Then Chester appeared from Maddy's room and started stalking him. *He isn't acting mean. I think he's trying to get Spunky's mind off of Henry.*

Spunky took the bait and chased Chester. After giving him some exercise, Chester jumped on the back of the sofa, too high for Spunky to reach. Spunky almost looked as though he was smiling. *He's enjoying this! Maybe he and Chester will be friends after all.*

Then Spunky lifted his leg, aiming for the leg of the sofa.

"Spunky, no!" She grabbed a handful of paper towels, then quickly snapped on his leash in case he wasn't done. When she returned, she grabbed her laptop and researched dog training. One book caught her eye. It was written by a monk living in upstate New York. At his monastery, they researched dog behavior and had developed a sound training method. *Maybe after lunch I can stop into the bookstore and see if they have this.* She could easily order it, but why pass up an excuse to browse through the bookstore?

Jessica was waiting under the green and white awning when Emily arrived at the Greenwood Café. Emily especially loved their vegetarian offerings, but seldom came down town for lunch. This would be a treat.

She hugged Jessica. "Jessica, that cast looks really uncomfortable. I'm surprised you were able to drive."

"Good thing it isn't my right arm. I wouldn't be able to get back and forth to work."

The café was painted light green with a white accent wall. The white wicker chairs and light wood tables gave the impression of perpetual summer. Emily watched a waitress carry an open-faced eggplant sandwich to a table.

"I'd forgotten how cute this place is," said Emily. "Look at those live flowers on the tables. Makes you forget it's the end of winter." She helped Jessica remove the coat she'd draped over her shoulders.

"Maddy can't stop talking about the new addition to your family."

"Spunky is adorable, though he needs a bit of training."

"Any news about the case?"

"Which case? The case of the man pushed off the roof in the middle of an arts festival, or the case of my sister, presumed dead for the last thirty years and suddenly spotted by a kidnapping victim?"

"Well, when you put it like that...I'm guessing nothing new about your sister since the trip was canceled."

"You guessed right."

"And the murder?"

"We know Toby Cutler was really Troy Cambridge. And his doctor down in Florida found his cardiac readout. Henry thinks his ICD was remotely activated, causing him to have a heart attack."

"His IC what?"

"An internal device that regulates heart rhythm. Kind of like a pacemaker."

"Then it wasn't murder after all?"

"Henry has a theory. He thinks Toby was too heavy to push off the roof so someone remotely caused him to have a heart attack, then led him to the edge."

"Then the killer may not have even been in the vicinity."

"No, there's a range. The murderer led Toby, I mean Troy, up to the rooftop. There were two sets of prints up there. One of which looked like muddy boots."

"Any guesses as to who?"

"Henry said that Toby was wearing work boots when he got to him. Those prints may have been his."

"The only one with a motive as far as we know is his son-in-law, Paul. But Paul has an alibi. Or so he says. I think he could have manipulated the alibi."

"It had to be someone knowledgeable about electronics, right?"

"Or computers. Paul works for a software company. I want to call Megan, but she's taking time off to get ready for her wedding. I don't want to bother her. And her partner is still on vacation, though he'll be back soon."

The waitress brought water. "Are you ready to order?"

Emily requested the eggplant sandwich while Jessica ordered a grilled chicken salad.

"Can you cut the pieces small? I'm not good with a knife right now."

The waitress glanced at the cast. "Of course."

"After lunch, do you want to come with me to the bookstore? I read about a dog training book I'd like to get my hands on."

"Sure. Might as well make the most of my sick day."

Neither Emily nor Jessica could finish their enormous portions. Emily took the bag of leftovers and popped it in the car before walking over to the bookstore.

"What's the book called?"

"*Being Your Dog's Best Friend*. There's the pet section." She fingered the spines of the books on the shelf. "There sure are a ton of books about dogs. I don't see it."

Jessica skimmed the bottom shelf. "Is this it?"

"Yes! Thanks."

Jessica read the back over Emily's shoulder. "Looks like it's based on being the dog's alpha figure."

"In that case, Henry better man up where Spunky's concerned." She read further. "Hey, this monastery isn't far from Watuga."

"When you go to pick up your sister, perhaps you can check it out," said Jessica.

"Maybe so. Meanwhile, I'll speedread the book before Henry gets home."

Chapter 23

As soon as Emily arrived home, read to curl up with her new book, Spunky whimpered at the door.

"You need to go out, don't you? At least you waited and let someone know." She put the leftovers in the fridge and grabbed the leash. "Come on."

It was chilly and she wished she hadn't left her gloves on the hall table. Spunky didn't mind the cold. He was taking his time sniffing every tree and licking up melted snow. Rebecca and Milo, her black and white Border Collie, came down the road. Milo was wearing a cable-knit sweater. Emily wondered if she should get a sweater for Spunky.

"Is this the new member of the Fox family?" said Rebecca. Milo and Spunky sniffed each other.

"Yes. Meet Spunky."

Rebecca bent down to pet him. "That's an appropriate name. Look how happy he is with that tail wagging and I think that's a smile."

I didn't know dogs were capable of smiling. I have a lot to learn. "He's very friendly. Loves Henry."

"I thought you were going out of town for a few days?"

"The lead didn't pan out. By the way, there have been some interesting developments in the murder case. First of all, the victim was using a false name and we don't know why. Secondly, it appears someone zapped into his heart device and then pushed him off the roof. Have you ever heard of such a thing?"

"You know I can't discuss my job at Biztech, but let's just say I know that kind of thing can be done. Fascinating."

Emily shivered. "I wish the police had some suspects or a motive. I think the son-in-law may be guilty."

"You look cold. Come inside."

Emily followed her. "It's okay to bring Spunky in?"

"Of course, it is. Now, if the victim was using an alias, he must have been hiding from someone or something. Either he knew someone was after him, or he needed to escape something he'd done."

"I googled Troy Cambridge, but couldn't even find which of the thousand Troy Cambridges was him. It's not an uncommon name."

"Do you mind if I try?"

"Please."

Rebecca said, "Has he always lived in Sugarbury Falls?"

"No. He moved here from Florida not more than a year ago."

"What was his job?"

"I'm not sure. Wait. Jessica said he worked as a security guard at the school where she teaches."

"Okay. Then he must have a gun permit, license…" She clicked keys while Emily looked over her shoulder.

"Emily, I hate to be like this, but some of these data bases aren't meant for the eyes of the general public."

She was slightly put off, but backed away. One day she'd love to know what kind of company Biztech was…if it was a company at all.

"Oh boy. Jackpot."

"What did you find?"

"Your Troy Cambridge was a security guard at a high school down in Canal Village, Florida. There was a mass shooting. You must remember when it was on the national news? Six students and two teachers were gunned down by a disgruntled ex-employee of the school system."

"Yes, I do remember. The students got together to change the gun laws."

"Yep. And there was a whole lot of controversy about the school, in particular, the security guard, not safeguarding the students. The guard was dragged through a nasty trial but eventually acquitted."

"Was it..."

"Troy Cambridge. And the timeline fits. He must have changed his name and moved far away to escape. It says here he was receiving death threats."

"That explains why he used a fake name, but do you think someone up here recognized him and took revenge?"

"Possibly."

"But who? One of the victim's family members? Or someone angry about the change in gun laws?"

"I don't know, but it shouldn't be hard for the police to check this out."

"Can you access the..." Spunky started whimpering and headed to the door. "I'd better get him outside fast. He hasn't gotten the potty-training down solidly yet. Thank you."

Spunky dribbled on every stick and leaf along the way back to the cabin. When they got back home, Emily flopped on the couch. *Ron Wooster should be back by tomorrow. I'm sure he can get the names of those students and teachers who were killed. I don't know what this world is coming to.* Her phone buzzed.

"Hi, Mom. Any news?"

"Nothing, but I'm getting impatient. I told Drew I want to ride up to Watuga anyway and see for myself."

"See what? We can't drive around the streets looking for a guy in camouflage with a parrot on his shoulder and a Down's syndrome girl—woman—by his side."

"It's a small town."

"But they could be long gone by now. Probably are, given the circumstances."

"I can't just sit by and wait."

"Did the PI turn up anything?"

"Not yet. Let's take a ride down there tomorrow. You were planning on being away."

"I'll have to clear it with Henry. I'll let you know." She knew Henry would be fine with it, but wasn't sure she wanted to make the trip without a solid lead.

She sat down to do some writing. *Troy was a security guard down in Florida. He was blamed for a mass shooting at a school. How could anyone believe a security guard would be a match for a lunatic with an assault weapon. Poor man.* Before she knew it, she heard both the school bus and Henry's car. Henry took off his jacket and threw his keys on the table. Maddy went directly into the kitchen.

"Henry, I found out a lot about Troy Cambridge this afternoon, thanks to Rebecca. He was a security guard in that Florida school where the mass shooting occurred. Canal Village High. Do you remember hearing about it in the news?"

"Yes, of course. Canal Village. Hmmm."

"Hmmm what?"

"When I was looking into Toby—Troy's—cardiac readout, the hospital where he had the surgery to implant the device was Canal Village General."

"That explains the name change. He was blamed for not stopping the shooting, there was a trial…"

"And he was acquitted. Probably hoped to come up here and retire in peace."

"Only, why did he take another job working security? Why not lay low and enjoy retirement?"

"With the cost of a trial, not to mention moving expenses coming here from Canal Village and lost wages while he awaited trial, maybe he needed the money."

"Okay, so we know why he was in Sugarbury Falls, why he changed his name, and how the murder was likely committed. Problem is, the police have no viable suspects."

Maddy came out from the kitchen holding a paper towel full of cookies.

"Hungry?" asked Henry.

"We eat lunch early at school. Did I hear you say Canal Village?"

"Yes, why?"

"Jessica's boyfriend, or ex-boyfriend, is from Canal Village."

Emily said, "Are you sure?"

"Yes. Don't you remember at the arts fair he saw those hand-made bleacher seats and he said he saw those a lot back in Canal Village?"

"I can't say I remember that comment, but I trust your memory," said Emily. "Sam said he had a daughter. I do remember that. Jessica thinks when his daughter died, that caused him to go off the deep end."

Henry said, "What if his daughter was one of the victims of the shooting? What if he followed Troy Cambridge here so he could get his revenge? Isn't he a technology teacher?"

"Yes, but he had a job with a technology company. Jessica thought he was lazy leaving it for teaching. Wouldn't he go after the shooter instead?" said Maddy.

Emily said, "The shooter was killed by the police during the incident. He needed to blame someone, and why not the security guard who he believes failed to protect his daughter?"

Henry said, "Give me a minute." He opened his laptop and did a search. "I've got the names of the victims here. There's a story about building a memorial wall and the names are engraved on it." He read the names aloud. "Tiffany Peters. I'll bet that's her."

"He had the knowledge to screw with the pacemaker."

Henry interjected. "The ICD. They're not the same."

"Okay, the ICD. I heard Toby/Troy being verbally attacked when I stopped to tie my shoe. Then, Sam disappeared. He joined us after we were all gathered by the roof."

"He caused the heart attack, pushed Toby off the roof, then ran down and joined the crowd. But how did he go unnoticed?"

"He didn't. A witness said they saw someone on the roof. And the muddy prints! It wasn't raining that day, but there's a path that goes behind the building. The sprinklers come on every afternoon at just about the time the murder happened. Sam ran down the back stairs, out the door, and onto the path behind the building."

Maddy said, "And that note was written in Expo marker. Sam's a teacher. He must use those all the time."

Spunky whimpered. Henry said, "See, he's saying he needs to go out."

"Only after he already peed on the floor. I bought a book today about how to train dogs. I'll let you read it."

Maddy spilled milk on her shirt. "I have to change."

Henry went out with Spunky. A few minutes later, Maddy ran into the living room. "Emily, we have to help. It's Jessica. She needs us."

"I was just with Jessica this afternoon."

"She called and said Sam was outside her door, threatening to kill her if she didn't open it. She thinks he has a gun."

Emily dialed the police station and reported it.

"Emily, let's go. What if he's already done something to her?"

"It could be dangerous if he has a gun."

"Exactly. She needs us."

"Let's wait for Henry."

"No, we have to get over there now!" Maddy ran out the door. Emily had no choice but to follow her. "If you don't drive us, I'll walk or hitch hike."

"Come on." Emily got into her Audi. "Text Henry and let him know what's going on." She prayed the police would be there before she and Maddy arrived.

"Can't you drive faster?"

"It's freezing rain. The roads are slippery."

"What if he's already killed her?"

Emily, laser focused, stepped on the gas. When they arrived at Jessica's, a police car was parked outside. Emily ran to the officer. "What's happening?"

"The guy busted the door open and now has her hostage inside. We're waiting for the special response unit."

"We have a special response unit here in Sugarbury Falls?"

"Yes. With what's been happening around the country, even small communities are able to get grants for these. Ours serves this whole northern quadrant of the state."

"Won't it take time?"

"A neighbor heard a gunshot before you called. They're on the way."

Another car pulled up. Emily recognized the detective. "Ron, I thought you were still on vacation until tomorrow?"

"Good thing I just got back in town and heard the call. Stay back, Emily."

Maddy ran over. "That's my sister in there. You have to help her."

"Here's the special response team now."

The special response team consisted of four men with shields and military grade weapons.

"Is that necessary?" asked Emily.

"It's a precaution. We'll try to end this peacefully, of course." He picked up a bull horn. "Sam, it's not too late to end this before anyone gets hurt. Let Jessica go. Come out with your hands up."

"What, or they'll shoot me? Like Troy Cambridge let that lunatic shoot my daughter?"

"What does Miss Pratt have to do with any of this?"

"She's not leaving me. My daughter is dead. My wife is gone. The loss split us apart. Jessica isn't leaving me. Do you hear me? I'll kill us both before that happens."

"We can get you help. I understand how devastating losing your daughter must have been, but Jessica shouldn't be punished. She's innocent."

"No, she isn't. I told you she wants to leave me. Over my dead body will that happen."

Maddy said, "Can I talk to him? Please?"

"Are you kidding?" said Emily.

"No. Stay back." Ron Wooster shooed them away.

Maddy took her phone out of her pocket and called Jessica's number. Sam picked up.

"Sam, please don't hurt my sister. You know how it feels to lose someone you love. My mother died recently. My father's in prison. Emily and Henry are great but I still mourn the loss of my biological family. Then Jessica came out of nowhere. A sister. My flesh and blood. If you kill her, I'll go through it all over again." She put the phone on speaker.

"Where's the violin music?"

"Wasn't your daughter about my age when she died? High school, right? You know how she would have felt if she was in my shoes right now facing the loss of a sister."

While she talked to him, the special response team entered through the back door. Emily's heart raced as she watched. She wanted to grab Maddy and whisk her home. A shot blasted from inside the house.

"Sam! Please, Sam. You didn't kill her, did you?" The silence was excruciating. Emily hugged Maddy. Ron Wooster ran toward the house just as the special response team came out with Sam, his hands over his head.

Maddy screamed. "Where's Jessica? Did he kill my sister? Where is she?"

Emily held her breath. Maddy ran toward the house.

"Maddy, stay here!" Emily started to run after her but an officer told her to stay put. He ran after Maddy, stopping her before she reached the door.

Finally, Ron Wooster exited, arm around Jessica, holding her steady. Maddy and Emily ran and hugged her.

Ron Wooster said, "Maddy, without you distracting Sam on the phone, this may have turned out much differently. You're a hero."

"I just wanted to save my sister. Jessica, are you hurt? We heard a shot."

"Sam's gun went off when he saw the special response team. Luckily, the shot went into the wall. I can't stop shaking."

"It's over," said Ron Wooster. "You're safe now. Maybe you should go to the hospital and get checked out. He lightly touched his fingers to the cast. "Did he hurt this arm?"

"Not any more than he did initially. I'm fine, really."

"Stay with us tonight," said Emily.

"No, I don't want to leave my kitten all alone. I'll be okay."

Henry pulled into the driveway. "What happened? I got home and everyone was gone. Then I turned on the TV and the story was all over the news. Jessica, are you okay?"

"I'm fine. Relieved that Sam can't hurt anyone anymore. I almost feel sorry for him."

Emily said, "I feel sorry for Toby Cutler. Poor man. Escaped being the scapegoat down in Florida only to be hunted down by a crazed father."

Chapter 25

Emily woke up to her phone buzzing on the nightstand, just as she did yesterday morning. She groped for it, knocking it to the floor, then stretching to pick it up.

"Mom, I was sleeping."

"Are you ready to go to New York and find Amy?"

"What?" She hadn't even remembered she'd been contemplating that. "We had a rough night."

"But I can't take it anymore. I have to find her."

"I thought the lead was a hoax? I can't afford to be away for more than a day or two."

"That's fine. Drew's PI thinks he has a lead."

"Another lead?"

"I don't have details but Drew and I said we'd meet him in New York."

"It's Thursday and Megan's wedding is Saturday. I can't afford to be away for more than a day or two."

"Please, Emily."

"I'll talk to Henry and call you back."

When Henry got back in with Spunky she explained the situation.

"We saw first-hand the bond between sisters with Maddy and Jessica last night. I know how you feel about Amy. Go ahead and see if the lead pans out."

"Are you sure?"

"Yes. Go. Just be back in time for the wedding."

Is this just a wild goose chase? I can't afford to get my hopes up and then be disappointed all over again. What if she really is alive? I have to find out. Emily called her mother and within half an hour she and Drew pulled into the driveway and honked for her.

The weather had cleared and for the first time in days, the sky was blue instead of gray. The ride seemed endless, but in reality, they reached Watuga by early afternoon.

"We're meeting the PI here but I'm not sure if we'll be driving further," said Frances.

They pulled into a diner and shortly afterwards, the PI arrived.

"What did you find? Do we need to keep going?"

"I'm sorry but the lead I was chasing didn't pan out. I'll keep working on it."

"What do you mean keep working on it? We drove all the way here anticipating good news."

"Like I said, I'm sorry."

"And you're fired," screamed Frances. She was in tears as soon as the PI left.

Emily felt her heart sink. *I should have known better.* Frances had tears in her eyes.

"Mom, as long as we're here, let's go to the police station. Maybe they have news."

"They don't. I call them every day. I just want to go home."

Drew said, "We'll have lunch and regroup. Here, look at the menu."

"I can't eat," said Frances.

Emily was starving. She never understood how people couldn't eat when stressed. She was just the opposite. "I'm going to get a veggie burger and fries. Mom, why don't you at least get a bowl of soup."

Frances agreed to soup. They were seated in a booth by the window. Emily saw a flyer on the window and tried to read it through the glass. The monks! It looked like an advertisement. The waitress came over to take their orders.

"Excuse me," said Emily. "What's that flyer on the window about?"

"The monks down the road are famous for their dog training methods. They run in-house obedience courses and operate a store that benefits the animals. It's become a bit of a tourist attraction. It's staffed by the monks and they're always willing to talk and give advice."

"And it's just down the road? Do you need to make an appointment?"

"No. Someone's always there at the store. They have several books out."

"I know. I just read one."

Drew cleared his throat. "I'll take the grilled cheese and tomato soup. My wife will have a bowl of the soup."

"Veggie burger for me," said Emily.

"Mom, Drew can we stop at the monastery on the way home? I'd love to ask a few questions."

Frances didn't say anything. Drew said, "Of course. Might as well get something out of this trip."

Watuga was somewhat of a tourist area in the summer but in winter, lacking ski facilities and lodges, it was quite desolate. The drive to the monastery was quick and signage led right to the door of the shop the waitress told them about.

"This is where you wanted to go?" said Frances.

"Yes." Emily pushed open the heavy wooden door and a bell chimed, signaling their arrival. It smelled like an old library, strangely pleasant and familiar. She wasn't sure what she had pictured, but the young, thin man behind the counter could pass for a tennis pro if not for the robe he wore. A Labrador was curled in a dog bed in the corner and the small shop was packed with dog toys, food, and an entire wall devoted to their publications. The latest book was stacked in a display near the door.

"Can I help you?"

Emily said, "Yes. I just finished reading your new book and had a few questions. We were in the area."

"Ask away."

"We adopted a three-legged mixed breed from the shelter. He's not a puppy, maybe two or three years old. He'd been caught in a bear trap and abandoned."

"Terrible. Those traps should be outlawed."

"He's been having accidents, yet sometimes goes to the door and whimpers to go out so we're not sure how much training he's had. My husband thinks it's cruel to put him in the crate. We tried and he kept whimpering until we took him out."

"Dogs are pack animals. They feel safe when they know their place in the family and will be most comfortable when they recognize an alpha figure."

"My husband?"

"Doesn't have to be a male. It's important to speak firmly, keep consistent, and reward positive behavior."

"Even if he whimpers?"

"He'll learn very quickly and he'll be a happier dog when he has clear rules to follow."

"Like children?"

"I suppose. Put him in his crate at night and whenever you go out, then immediately take him out for a walk when you return. Oh, and when you are home, don't give him free reign of the house. Confine him to a smaller area. Pretty soon he'll go in the crate by choice, you'll see."

"Thank you. I'll relay all of this to my husband."

"We run in-residence obedience training sessions if you find it necessary. We also have a free podcast." He handed her a card.

Emily picked up a bag of treats from the counter. "So all the monks are dog experts?"

"It's certainly our focus, but one of the brothers has a dozen cats he feeds and in the cold months he keeps them in the barn."

The bell chimed and a stout, older monk entered. "Welcome, friends. Brother Tony, do we have any more of the wild bird seed in the back?"

"Yes. I saw some this morning on the shelf under the dog treats. Speaking of experts, we refer to brother Michael here as the bird man. He can tell you anything and everything about birds."

"Really?" said Emily. "What do you know about parrots?"

"Where to start. There are many varieties of parrots, but in general, they live long lives—upwards of seventy years if well cared for. This isn't their preferred climate, but as indoor pets they can thrive just about anywhere."

"I guess you don't see a whole lot of those around here, especially in winter."

"You'd be surprised. Just now I heard one when I was out walking. When I got closer, I saw it was with a couple out gathering firewood. We're expecting a storm later today. Sat right on the man's shoulder."

Emily's heart felt as though it stopped mid-beat. "A couple with a parrot? What did they look like?"

"Well, the blond lady was heavy set, not old but not young."

"And the man?"

"Older, with a long beard. He was wearing an army jacket and beret."

"Do you remember exactly where you saw them?"

"When you go out the door, instead of heading to the parking lot, you follow the path around back which leads to the woods. They were only about a mile in from here."

Frances grabbed Emily's arm. "Can you point us in the right direction?"

Drew said, "Can we drive back there?"

"You can't drive, it's too narrow."

Emily paid for the dog treats. "Thank you."

"Glad we could help."

"You've been more help than I could have imagined, "said Emily.

Chapter 26

"We have to tell the police," said Drew.

"Why? They won't take us seriously," said Frances.

"We can't go chasing them alone. What if he's got a shotgun?"

Emily said, "I'm going to call my friend Susan Wiles. If her detective daughter makes the call, they'll listen." She sounded braver than she felt. She took her phone out of her pocket. *Answer, Susan. Come on.* The phone rang three times. *Maybe I hit the wrong number.* Emily was about to give up when she heard her friend's voice.

"Susan, thank God. It's Emily. I need your help…"

Frances, who'd been pacing in circles while Emily called, grabbed her arm. "Let's go before they disappear."

They slipped into the murky woods behind the monastery. Emily stepped over fallen branches and pine needles. She was confident she could easily walk a mile or more, but worried it would be difficult for her mother and Drew. What choice did they have? The sky, robin's egg blue on the way to Watuga, had turned steely gray.

"What did Susan say?" said Frances.

"She'll call Lynette immediately. I gave her the monk's directions." They stomped over dry branches, the sound echoing in the quiet, natural sanctuary. Her feet were mini icicles inside her damp canvas sneakers; Emily wished she'd opted instead for her slightly uncomfortable boots. "I'll call Henry to let him know what's going on." She tried multiple times then threw her phone into the snow. "No service! Good thing I got Susan. A few minutes later and no one would know where we are."

Drew retrieved the phone. "Let's move before we get further behind." They trudged along the path. Frances lagged behind. "Mom, want to stop and rest a little?"

"No, I'm okay. We have to find her."

"Look," said Drew. He ran his hand over a knotty trunk. "These trees have fresh cuts. See the missing branches?"

Frances said, "How do you know?"

"Boy Scouts. All the way to Eagle Scouts in fact."

"You continue to surprise me," said Frances. "Ouch."

"Mom, what's wrong?"

"Nothing. I just stepped the wrong way. Come on."

They continued. Emily watched her mother limp, not putting her full weight down on the ankle. "Mom, maybe we should go back. It looks like you're having trouble walking."

"My ankle got a little twisted, but that's not going to stop me from finding my daughter." She picked up a large branch. "Now I've got my own cane. Let's go."

Flurries swirled between the fragrant pines. Emily couldn't feel her cheeks. Even using the branch to lean on, her mother was falling behind. "Mom, maybe we should go back?" She bent down and gently pulled up her mother's pant leg. "It's already swelling."

"I'll be fine. Are those more cut trees?"

Drew ran his hand along the bark. "You're a quick learner. Yes, they are."

"Which way?"

They stood still. A sound. A cawing sound. A parrot sound?

Frances said, "It's a parrot! I hear a parrot."

Drew said, "It could just be an owl."

"Don't they sleep by day?" said Emily. They heard the sound again. "It's a parrot. Mom's right. It came from that direction."

They went deeper into the woods, stopping every few feet to listen.

"I don't hear it anymore," said Frances. "What if they've gone inside?"

"Inside where? We haven't passed any cabins," said Emily.

Drew said, "Listen."

"All I hear is the wind whistling," said Emily.

"No. There. Hear it? It's coming from behind those trees. Come on." The biting air blew snow in their faces. Emily felt both worried and impatient. Her mother, leaning on the branch, reminded her of Spunky following Henry, only Spunky was much quicker.

"Mom, should we go back?"

"No, of course not. I'm fine." Drew offered her his arm.

Emily felt frustrated, wanting to run but having to wait for her mother to keep up.

"It sounds closer. Much closer," said Frances.

"There!" said Emily. She trembled from head to toe as she saw a man in camouflage with a parrot on his shoulder. Then she noticed a woman holding an armful of branches, blond hair poking out of her ski cap. She couldn't move. "It's Amy." She felt as though she was about to faint.

Frances grabbed her arm. "I...I can hardly breathe. It's her. Let's go."

"Wait!" said Drew. "What if he has a gun?"

"Gun? Seriously? He can't be holding a gun. He's holding a chain saw!"

"Even worse!"

"What should we do?"

Emily tried her phone again. Still no service.

"I'm going to go to Amy," said Frances. She took a few shaky steps.

"Mom, no. She won't remember you and she'll be scared."

Drew said, "He's holding a chain saw. Have you never seen a horror movie?"

"She hasn't forgotten me. I'm sure of it." She hobbled out from behind the tree. "Amy. It's me. It's Mommy! Come here, baby."

Amy and the man spun around. The parrot cawed. The man yelled, "Go away. You're not taking us alive!" He turned on the saw.

Frances screamed over the sound. "Amy, we love you. Please, come to me."

Amy looked back and forth between Frances and the man in camouflage. The man turned off the saw so he could be heard. "You're not taking her prisoner. Don't come any closer. Nan nhân, go back to the tent. It's the enemy."

He stepped toward them. "Run, Nan nhân, and get the ammo ready." He turned the saw back on, holding it like a gun.

Amy turned and started to run away. Emily had an idea.

She began to sing. Her voice strained over the sound of the saw but she'd do anything to be heard. *"I'm gonna wash that man right out of my hair. I'm gonna wash that man right outta my hair."* She took a few steps closer. *"I'm gonna wash that man right outta my hair."*

Amy stared at Emily, then looked back and forth between her and Frances. Then she smiled and sang. *"I'm gonna wash..."*

Emily sang along with her, both crooning over the buzz of the chainsaw. *"That man right outta my hair and send him on his way."* Amy ran to her. It was a hug like no other. After all these years, after thinking she was gone forever, Emily embraced her sister, hugging her close against her heart. "Amy, I love you. I missed you so much." Tears streamed down her face—down both their faces.

Amy, head on Emily's shoulder said, "I love you, Em & Em."

Frances fell into the embrace, Drew stood behind her holding his phone in different positions, searching for reception.

"I love you, Mommy."

The man had been coming toward them, stalking like a hungry tiger. "Nan nhân come here now! That's the enemy you're talking to. They're trying to capture you. Come here." He strode closer to them.

Amy broke away and stood between her loved ones and her captor.

"Come, sweetheart. Let's take you home." Frances hobbled toward her, then fell into the snow. Drew helped her up.

"Mom, we have to get you to a hospital."

"Not until Amy is safe with us. Amy, come back to Mommy."

Amy looked at Frances, then at the man. "No. Not without Poppy." She ran to Poppy who yelled, "retreat." She disappeared into the forest. Poppy stepped backwards into the woods, shielding himself with the buzzing chain saw. Then, the chain saw fell silent.

"I'll bet it's out of gas." Drew tried the police. "Still no phone reception."

When Poppy realized he no longer had a weapon, he ran into the woods.

Emily called out to Amy "Come with us and we'll come back for Poppy later."

She ran into the woods, frustrated that she couldn't find Amy. Then, she heard Amy's voice calling, "Poppy, where are you? Dorian. Here, Dorian." Amy emerged from behind a clump of trees.

"Amy, Poppy is sick. Let's get him a doctor. Come with us."

Amy stopped and looked back and forth between the woods and Emily. Then she took a step toward Emily. "You'll help him?"

"Yes, of course."

"Pinky swear?"

"Pinky swear." In reality, she vowed to herself to have him thrown in jail for the rest of his life but she'd say anything to keep Amy safe.

They went back to Frances and Drew. Drew had taken off his coat and spread it on the ground so Frances could sit. He stuffed snow inside his scarf and tied it around her ankle. "This should help the swelling."

Amy said, "We have to get Dorian."

Frances said, "Who's Dorian?"

Amy answered. "He's our birdie. Come here, Dorian."

Fine pellets of snow clung to Amy's cap. "Let's go before we get stranded," said Emily. Although Drew assured her Poppy had run deeper into the woods, the frozen hairs on her arms prickled as though the threat was waiting around the corner. "Let's hurry, Amy. We can get hot chocolate and cookies at home."

Drew helped Frances to her feet, shook out his coat, and wrapped it over her.

"Let's go. Poppy and Dorian will be safe and warm until we come back for them."

Amy responded to Drew's authoritative command and walked with them.

Amy looked at Emily, her eyes begging to believe Drew. "They'll be safe and warm? We'll come right back for them?"

"Yes, honey." Emily felt the warmth of Amy's pudgy hand through her mittens as she squeezed it. Frances and Drew were already lagging behind. "You have to meet Maddy. You have a niece. She's fourteen." *The age you were when I last saw you.* "And we have a black cat named Chester."

"Dorian doesn't like cats."

"Everyone loves Chester. And we just got a new dog."

"I love dogs. Did you name him Snoopy?"

"His name is Spunky. He walks on three legs."

Amy giggled. "Like a sack race. Remember, Emily? We won."

"We sure did." She was relieved to hear Amy had clear memories from before they were separated.

"We can have hot chocolate?"

"And cookies." They were almost back to where they'd parked the car when Emily froze. Drew and Frances caught up to them.

"Did you hear something?"

Frances said, "Only the wind."

"I guess you're right." They continued. Emily stopped again and said, "You didn't hear that just now?"

"Maybe."

Emily screamed. "No!"

Poppy leaped at Amy from behind a tree. Emily punched at him but through the padding of his jacket it hadn't made any impact. He kicked her in the shins, causing her to fall in the snow, then dragged Amy back toward the woods.

"Stop!" Emily scrambled up and ran at him. He waved a silver blade back and forth, slashing through the gray sky. Her heart felt like a wild animal trying to burst through her chest. *Stay calm. You have to think.*

"I'd turn around if I were you. My men have this place covered. They're hiding behind the rocks. They're hiding in the trees."

What men? He's hallucinating. Fight or flight? Fight. Emily charged at him.

Poppy pushed Amy away and grabbed Emily.

"Amy!" Emily took a step in her direction but felt paw-like hands squeeze her from behind. She felt the icy blade of the knife against her neck. She couldn't breathe. It would be impossible to escape his grip without the knife slashing her throat.

Drew ran toward him. "Drop it and let her go!"

Poppy let out an actual roar. His face contorted into an ugly mask of evil. "Take another step and she's dead."

Frances wailed. "Amy, come here."

Ignoring her mother, Amy didn't miss a beat. She fled toward Poppy, then disappeared into the woods.

Poppy said to Frances and Drew, "Turn around and keep walking. I'm taking the prisoner. Take a step toward me and she's dead." Holding Emily, he backed up into the woods. Emily was still unable to move and couldn't think of any way to escape. She tried to drop to the ground, becoming dead weight in his grasp. He slowed down, but not by much.

Emily thought about Maddy and Henry waiting at home for her. They had no idea she may never return. And what about Chester? Her heart ached at the thought of never seeing them again.

"I've hidden explosives allover these woods. You'd better hope they don't try to follow us." He zig-zagged through the woods as if avoiding certain parts of the path. "The prison isn't far." His strength surprised her.

He's crazy. He thinks he's back in Vietnam. I'll bet he fought there.

"The enemy must retreat!"

Emily heard a thump, saw a flash of metal, and felt Poppy's grip loosen. Seizing the opportunity, she unclenched his fingers from around her neck and pulled free. He collapsed into a heap on the snowy ground. Amy stood over him, shovel in hand.

"Amy! You saved my life."

"I love you, Em&Em. I washed him out of my hair."

"Yes, you sure did. Come on before he wakes up."

Amy grasped her sister's hand. She clung to it as they trudged backed toward the monastery to where they'd parked the now snow-coated car. Drew brushed off the windshield as they huddled together.

"I have to call Henry," said Emily. "I'd better get reception here."

Drew said, "You have to alert the police as well. If they act fast, they should be able to apprehend Poppy."

Sirens blared. Then they saw red and blue lights racing toward them. Frances said, "Looks like someone already alerted them."

A female with a blond ponytail jumped out of the cruiser. "Emily? Are you okay?"

"Lynette. I knew your mom would come through for us."

"The monks contacted the local police. When I called the Watuga station, they were already heading here. Thank goodness you are all safe."

"He's still out there in the woods. My mother needs a doctor."

"He won't get far. The canine unit is already searching."

"Lynette, this is my sister, Amy. She saved my life just now."

Chapter 27

Sunlight streamed through the stained glass windows and organ music echoed through the church. Maddy whispered to Emily. "I'm nervous. What if I trip?"

"You won't. Come on. That's our cue." She and Maddy, along with Megan's friend Kim, started down the aisle. Emily smiled at Henry waiting at the end of the aisle next to Pat. Pat glowed with such an abundance of happiness that she felt it radiating as they approached. Last time they'd all been together in this church was for Carol's funeral. Emily felt Carol's presence. Not weak and sick like in her last days, but healthy and happy, smiling down—giving them her blessing.

The congregation rose and Megan took center stage, absolutely gorgeous in a silk gown that floated behind her as she walked toward her future. Her hair was half up under the lacy veil, with tendrils of red curls cascading down her back and framing her face.

The ceremony was traditional, yet personal. Megan and Pat had written additional vows and Emily fought to keep her mascara from running down her face as they tenderly shared them. She even spotted tears in Henry's eyes.

"I now pronounce you husband and wife."

Pat and Megan kissed, then they exited the church.

Henry said to Emily, "Did you bring rice?"

"Birdseed," said Maddy. "No one throws rice anymore."

"When did you become an etiquette expert?" said Henry. They joined the reception line outside the church then drove to the Tory House.

Henry, Maddy, and Emily sat with Jessica, Coralee, and her son, Noah. Blue ribbons adorned the chairs, matching the ribbons tying together the wild flower centerpieces.

"This place is gorgeous," said Coralee. "Megan and Pat look so happy. And there's her partner, Ron Wooster, congratulating them. What a handsome young man. I hope his vacation helped."

"What do you mean, helped?" asked Emily.

"His girlfriend dumped him for a traveling salesman who was passing through town. Just like that after dating a whole year. He's better off without her."

"A traveling salesman?"

"Well, technically. He was a drug rep for a pharmaceutical company."

Jessica said, "I can relate. You think you know someone, and bam. Poor Ron. He was so sweet when he rescued me from Sam the other day. Even called to check up on me later that evening."

Coralee said, "He's a good man. I've known him since he was a baby."

Emily's phone vibrated. "Aww. Speaking of babies, look. Lisa Cutler just sent this picture of her new grandson. Shari had her baby this morning. Anthony Troy, seven pounds, eight ounces."

She showed the picture to Coralee. "He's adorable."

Maddy said, "Kittens are so much cuter than babies."

Henry took out his phone. "If you really want to see cute, look at this picture of Spunky."

Coralee said, "By the way, how's Amy doing? She's been very quiet at the inn. Beautiful smile, though. Emily, you must be so thrilled."

"She's doing okay, but she keeps asking about Poppy and Dorian."

"Dorian?"

"The parrot. He's getting the once over from the vet and believe it or not, mom agreed to let Amy keep him once he gets a clean bill of health. Frances and Drew will take Amy and Dorian home with them and will get counseling. I can hardly bear the thought of them taking her away."

Henry said, "Drew and Frances were in the process of moving. They are tossing around the idea of living here in Sugarbury Falls."

"Why was she taken?" asked Noah. "And kept alive all those years?"

Emily said, "As far as the police have gathered, Poppy is a Vietnam vet. When he returned home, his wife had left him and he struggled to find a job. He suffers from severe PTSD."

Henry continued. "He told the police he was protecting Amy from the enemy—the North Vietnamese. Apparently he'd stashed away food and supplies in the cabin that burned down. Told them it was his bunker and he was going to keep Amy—Nan nhân—safe."

Emily added, "That's why he kidnapped the other girl. He thought he was rescuing her from the enemy as well."

Coralee said, "Did you say non-young?"

"Sounds that way. It's actually Nan nhân. It's a Vietnamese term for someone you protect and keep safe," said Emily. "I wonder what will happen to him."

Detective Ron Wooster joined them. "Gregory Cole—Poppy—will most likely be placed in a mental facility to get the help he needs. After talking to your friend's daughter and the Watuga detectives, I doubt they'll find him capable of standing trial."

"Lynette was a big help. If I hadn't called Susan when I did, the police wouldn't have been in the area, ready to chase down Poppy. Mental facility? I'm sorry, but after what he did, we're going to push for a trial. He deprived me of my sister for all those years. Not to mention the horrible guilt I've dealt with every day since."

The lights dimmed. It was time for the first dance. "Megan and Pat couldn't look more in love," said Jessica.

Emily whispered in her ear. "You'll find that, too. Now that Sam is out of your life, you're free to get on with yours. Maybe sooner than you think."

Ron Wooster whispered. "Jessica, you're looking better. I mean, you look beautiful. The other day at the house, you know…" He stumbled over his words.

"I hadn't brushed my hair what with the shotgun aimed at my head and all."

"I didn't mean…"

"I know. I'm kidding. You look better all cleaned up too. I mean, not that you weren't clean. It's just…the suit and all."

"Jessica?" Ron shifted his weight from one foot to the other.

"Yes?"

"Um…Would you like to dance?"

Jessica smiled. "I'd love to."

THE END

ABOUT THE AUTHOR

 Diane Weiner is a public school teacher and mother of four children. She has enjoyed reading for as long as she can remember. She has fond memories of reading Nancy Drew and Mary Higgins Clark on snowy weekend afternoons in upstate New York and yearned to write books that would bring that kind of enjoyment to her readers. Being an animal lover, she is a vegetarian and shares her home with two adorable cats. In her free time, she enjoys running, attending community theater productions, and spending time with her family (especially going to the mall with her teenage daughter and getting Dairy Queen afterwards).

The Muddy Course is the fifth in Diane's Sugarbury Falls series. The first book in this series, *A Deadly Course*, recently received an Eric Hoffer International Book Competition Finalist Award for general fiction. The second is *Murder, of Course,* the third is *Clearing the Course*, and the fourth is *The Tainted Course*.

Diane also writes the Susan Wiles Schoolhouse mysteries.

Visit dianeweinerauthor.com to find out more about the author.

OTHER BOOKS BY DIANE WEINER

Murder is Elementary
Murder is Secondary
Murder in the Middle
Murder is Private
Murder is Developmental
Murder is Legal
Murder is Collegiate
Murder is Chartered
Murder is Homework

A Deadly Course
Murder, of Course
Clearing the Course
The Tainted Course

www.ingramcontent.com/pod-product-compliance
Lightning Source LLC
Chambersburg PA
CBHW030117260626
47156CB00008B/2699